Book One
The Summer of Magic Quartet

The White Horse Talisman

Andrea Spalding

Orca Book Publishers

National Library of Canada Cataloguing in Publication Data
Spalding, Andrea.
The white horse talisman

(The summer of magic quartet; bk. 1)
ISBN 1-55143-187-4 (bound) — 1-55143-222-6 (pbk.)

I. Title.
PS8587.P213W44 2001   jC813'.54   C2001-910959-8   PZ7.S7319Wh 2001

First published in the United States, 2002

Library of Congress Catalog Card Number: 2001092686

Orca Book Publishers gratefully acknowledges the support for our publishing programs provided by the following agencies: The Government of Canada through the Book Publishing Industry Development Program (BPIDP), The Canada Council for the Arts, and the British Columbia Arts Council.

Cover design: Christine Toller
Cover and interior illustrations: Martin Springett
Printed and bound in Canada

IN CANADA:
Orca Book Publishers
PO Box 5626, Station B
Victoria, BC Canada
V8R 6S4

IN THE UNITED STATES:
Orca Book Publishers
PO Box 468
Custer, WA   USA
98240-0468

03   02   01 • 5 4 3 2

Dedicated to Gavin and Janet Clarke, a much loved brother and sister-in-law. For years they uncomplainingly hosted our many trips to England, providing beds, food, laughter, love, and the loan of a car. They even hid their sighs of relief as we drove off on our travels! Thanks — this book is one of the results.

Acknowledgements

As always, many people helped me research and write this book. I would particularly like to thank my husband Dave, who encouraged and helped me along every step of the magical journey and found incredible research material. Our friend Tim Sands was an entertaining and knowledgeable companion on one of our research trips, and took some terrific photos. Special thanks to Professor Paul Smith of Memorial University, who was able to locate *The Scouring of the White Horse* by Thomas Hughes, and to Professor Bill Sarjeant, who lent his copy of S.G. Wildman's *The Black Horsemen*.

The amazing women in my life are always a source of support. My daughter Penny patiently read and commented on my many (many) drafts, Cheryl Oke several times provided wonderful meals on days she sensed I was snowed under, and fellow writers Sheryl MacFarlane and Georgina Montgomery always provided an ear and advice when I hit a problem. Thanks also to all the members of my family, who shower me with love and approval (even on days I forget they are coming) and provide grandchildren who ask for another book.

Grateful thanks to the Orca pod for its support and encouragement on what has turned out to be a long-term project, and to Canada Council and BC Arts Council for their support.

NOTE: Celtic spelling was used for two names in the story. "Myrddin" is pronounced "merthin" and "Halydd" is pronounced "halith." "Traa dy liooar" is Manx, the Celtic language of the Isle of Man. It means "time enough" and is pronounced "trae de lure."

Table of Contents

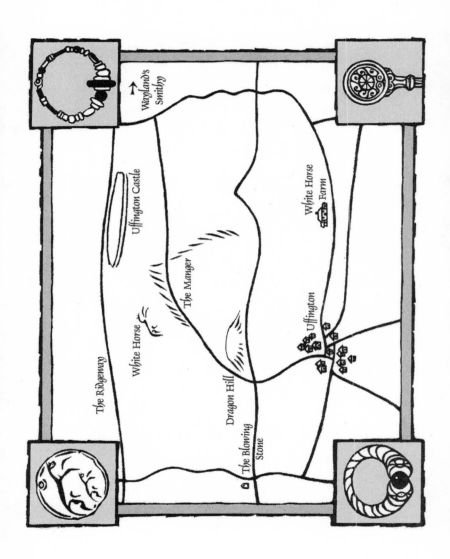

THE WISE ONES

Before the gods that made the gods
Had seen their sunrise pass,
The White Horse of the White Horse Vale
Was cut out of the grass.

from *The Ballad of the White Horse*
– G.K. Chesterton

In the Place Beyond Morning, terrible trouble arose.

The Dark Being marshaled her forces and stood before the great Gates of Sunrise, poised to seize power.

Inside the silver citadel the Wise Ones held council.

The Lady fingered the heavy turquoise, amber, and colored glass necklace around her throat, and watched while the tools of power were laid on the stone table before her.

Equus dislodged the gold talisman from his forelock,

Myrddin surrendered his staff, and Ava lowered her head so the silver circlet could be removed. The three objects were placed reverently before the Lady.

"Without these tools of power, the Dark Being will find victory brings nothing," said the Lady.

"Destroy these, and we are nothing," responded Equus.

The Lady gave a smile as brilliant as sunshine. "Not destroy, conceal."

Three pairs of eyes stared at her.

"In a galaxy known as the Milky Way spins Gaia, an almost unnoticed misty blue planet. On it are many places of great beauty, among them an island known as Angel Land after the fair-haired race that inhabits it. Those people will honor your tools and keep them safe. The talisman, staff, and circlet will be hidden in the center of Angel Land."

"And the necklace, Lady?" Myrddin asked.

"That I must guard. A smaller isle lies off the coast of Angel Land. It is home of a mage called Manannin who keeps his island hidden within a cloak of mist. I will hide there.

"Go swiftly and safely on the wings of dawn, my friends. Conceal your magic tools in Angel Land, trust in the humans, then leap for the stars to watch over them."

"Come with us, Lady," Ava pleaded.

The Lady shook her head. "The necklace and I must sleep behind Manannin's cloak. As long as the beads and I stay linked, so shall the magic link us all."

"We must help Angel Land keep the old magic alive," warned Myrddin.

Ava and Equus nodded agreement.

A gigantic roar erupted as the forces of the Dark Being battered the Gates of Sunrise.

"Fly!" cried the Lady. "All others are gone from our citadel. Only we remain." She stretched out her arms in blessing. "Traa dy liooar, let there be time enough."

The great gates shattered behind them as the four leapt for the stars.

So the Wise Ones departed the Place Beyond Morning. Hiding among sunbeams and traveling along moonbeams, they hurtled through galaxies towards the misty blue planet and Angel Land.

Foiled, the Dark Being vowed to search to the ends of time for the objects of power.

Ages passed.

In Angel Land, the people welcomed the Wise Ones and created ceremonial places to honor the magical tools entrusted to them.

The talisman was held by the People of the Horse, who rode the valleys between the chalk downs. They carved a great white horse to honor Equus.

Ava's circlet was concealed within a small sanctuary guarded by a henge of stones.

Myrddin's staff was laid to rest at the center of a labyrinth. A mountainous tor was raised to protect the spot.

Behind Manannin's cloak of mist the Lady slumbered. A castle rose over her resting place.

3

In the way of all things, the centuries moved forward and memories faded. The angel-haired people passed into the mists of time. The name of their land became England, not Angel Land. The Wise Ones' tools were forgotten, and the old magic dwindled into fragments of songs and stories remembered by children. Only the ceremonial places remained. Though their meaning was lost, they were admired as curiosities from a bygone age.

The vanquished Wise Ones watched from the stars while the Lady slept. To keep the old magic alive, they chose children and whispered to them in dreams. But as the years slipped by, fewer and fewer children heard their voices.

One day the fabric of the universe shuddered. The Dark Being and her forces entered the Milky Way.

The Wise Ones showered the misty blue planet with star messages and warnings. The people below admired the celestial fireworks but did not understand their meaning. The Wise Ones were near despair. Without human help, their tools would be lost forever. They sent another shower of star messages.

One was witnessed by a seven-year-old child who still believed in dreams.

ONE FOR SORROW

It was seven minutes after midnight.

Chantel Maxwell couldn't sleep. She was exhausted from the long plane journey from Canada, but her mind buzzed with excitement and worry.

"Four weeks in England, without Mom and Dad," she murmured, turning her head to find a cool spot on the pillow. "But I like White Horse Farm." She closed her eyes and tried to sleep. It was no use; she was wide awake.

Chantel slid out of bed and tiptoed over the floorboards. They creaked and groaned. She glanced towards her cousin. Eleven-year-old Holly lay sprawled across the next bed. She did not stir. Chantel slipped between the curtains and leaned out of the window beneath the thatched roof of the old farmhouse.

The night was filled with magic. She breathed deeply, trying to place the smells of the English countryside. The aroma of chickens and geese and the musky scent of horse wafted up from the pasture. A clean, green-smelling breeze rolled down from the hills her cousins called the downs. The full moon gleamed, throwing everything into sharp relief, so different from Edmonton, the Canadian city where she lived with her brother Adam.

"Blue shadows," Chantel murmured in surprise. "And stars ... so close." She lifted up her hand to the sky as if to touch one.

Whooooosh.

A flash of light streaked the night.

Chantel almost tumbled out of the open window in excitement. "A shooting star ... a real shooting star ... It landed up there!" She craned her neck to check the downs beyond the farm, where an ancient white horse was carved into the hillside, a magical horse carved through the grass into the white chalk so long ago that no one could remember how or why. The shooting star had aimed straight for it.

It was seven minutes after midnight, on the seventh day.

The shooting star touched the white horse. Brilliant blue light flickered across the chalk carving.

Chantel sighed dreamily, "If that was a magic star, I'd wish the White Horse would come to life."

The blue light grew stronger and a ghostly horse shook itself free of the chalk. Equus paused, absorbing the moonlight and growing more substantial. He was a king among horses, with flared nostrils and starlit eyes blazing with intelligence. The sculptured head turned from side to side. At last! A Magic Child was near. He could sense it. Ears flickered, and the spun-silver mane and tail lifted in the breeze. Muscles rippled solidly beneath his skin. Equus tossed his head and whinnied, then pawed the ground seven times, raising a shower of silvery sparks.

No one answered. The child did not yet know of her magic. He must wait. Equus bunched his powerful haunches and with a great leap galloped across the midnight sky in a flurry of moonbeams.

I must be dreaming, Chantel thought, and tiptoed back to bed with a smile of wonder on her lips.

It was seven minutes after midnight, on the seventh day of the seventh month. The witness was seven-year-old Chantel, who did not understand.

No matter. It was enough. The summer of magic could begin.

◆ ◆ ◆

"Come on, you lot, get up," Owen called. He grinned at Adam and pounded a wicked tattoo on the girls' bedroom door before clattering downstairs, laughing.

Adam and Owen had been up for ages. They'd collected eggs from the chickens, admired the racehorses, fed carrots to the ponies and been chased by the geese.

They erupted hungrily into the kitchen.

"Breakfast's ready. Tell your sisters," Uncle Ron said as he juggled slices of bread and a large frying pan full of bacon.

"Breakfast time, come and get it," bellowed Owen from the bottom of the stairs.

Dressed and ready for action, Holly ran down, but several minutes passed before a sleepy Chantel entered the kitchen.

"Chantel! You're still in PJs." Adam Maxwell looked at his little sister with disgust. "We've been up for hours." He grinned across at Owen and took a huge bite of his sandwich.

Chantel stood beside Uncle Ron. "Sandwiches? For breakfast?"

"Not sandwiches. Bacon and egg butties, an English treat." Uncle Ron flipped an egg out of the fry pan and flopped it onto a big slice of homemade bread covered with bacon. He slapped a second slice of bread on top, cut the sandwich in half and handed the plate to Chantel.

The egg yolk oozed enticingly and the smell of the bacon made her mouth water. Chantel sat at the table and took a bite.

"This is good." Suddenly she was ravenous and wolfed it down.

Holly grinned across at Owen. "It's the first day of the summer with our cousins. What shall we do?"

"Can we go to see that white horse carved in the grass?" asked Adam.

Chantel stopped eating as a fuzzy memory tugged at the back of her mind. "I dreamed about a horse ... a white horse ... last night," she said softly.

As usual, Adam ignored her. "Can we hike up there?" he asked.

"Great idea," said Holly excitedly. "We'll show you the White Horse and the old Iron Age fort on the top of the hill."

"Let's ride up." Owen looked at Adam, then towards Chantel. "Can you ride? Can she?"

"I can ride." Chantel was hurt. "We've been trail riding in the Rockies. I love riding, don't I, Adam?"

"Guess so," Adam said. He turned to Uncle Ron. "She rides a bit, but I've taken lessons. Can we ride the race-horses? They're cool!"

Uncle Ron laughed. "Definitely not! They are highly strung speed machines only exercised by their trainers. You kids are welcome to use the ponies, as long as you are sensible ... but don't forget your riding hats."

"We don't have any." Chantel was worried.

"There are lots in the tack room. One will fit," Holly said, licking egg off her fingers.

Uncle Ron squeezed Holly's and Owen's shoulders. "Remember your cousins are not used to riding all day. Take it easy. You've got a whole month together."

The kids rolled their eyes and left the kitchen.

⊠ ⊠ ⊠

Adam almost tripped over his little sister on the stairs. Chantel was sitting on the top step, staring into space.

"What's up with you?" Adam said.

Chantel shook her head. "Nothing, just waiting for Holly."

Adam bent down and stuck his face into Chantel's. "Listen, you, this is my holiday. You weren't coming until Mom stuck her oar in, so it's still my holiday with Owen. No messing it up. Mom and Dad shipped you out of their way, but you're not going to get in mine. Understand?"

Chantel's lip trembled, but she stuck out her chin determinedly. "Mom and Dad didn't want you around either," she retorted.

Adam flushed. "Who cares? They're just nuts. Always fighting. I'm glad they're not here. Owen and I have plans this summer, and you better not mess with them." He pushed past her.

Chantel sighed.

The afternoon was hot and sticky — the sort that ends with a storm. Owen, Adam, Holly, and Chantel ignored the heat. They had taken their time exploring the roads around the farm and village, but now trotted briskly along the Ridgeway, the narrow track that wound along the crest of the downs. Adam chattered away to Holly and Owen, ignoring his sister.

For once, Chantel didn't mind. She was gripped by the strange feeling of being pulled forward, drawn up the Ridgeway by an invisible thread. She leaned over her pony's neck and urged it on. "Come on, Snowflake." She edged ahead of the older kids, humming a little song under her breath.

"She's happy." Owen jerked his head towards Chantel.

Adam laughed. "She's weird. She lives in a dream world. I bet she thinks she's a princess or something." He looked up at the sky. It was a dull, hazy blue. The air felt hot and thundery. "Is there going to be a storm?"

Holly glanced around. "Maybe. But we're not far from

home." She kicked Harlequin's side and caught up to Chantel.

Chantel strained forward. The dream horse memory was clear in her mind. As she approached the carving she could hear it calling, a whinnying song urging her uphill. As the pony carried her closer, the horse's voice grew stronger.

Humming her own song back, Chantel leaned forward to pat her pony's neck. Snowflake whickered softly in response.

"You okay?" asked Holly as she and Harlequin drew level.

The question brought Chantel back to reality for a moment. She nodded, gave Holly an excited smile, then strained forward again.

Holly stared at the younger girl.

Under her hat, Chantel's small face was rosy with effort. Damp tendrils of red hair were plastered against her cheekbones.

"Are you too hot?" Holly asked. "We can go back if you like. We can always come up another day, when it's cooler."

Chantel looked at her cousin with surprise. "Go back?" she said. "No way! I'm nearly at the White Horse."

They passed a small tree. Chattering with alarm, a large blue-black bird with white markings flew across the track.

"One for sorrow," Holly muttered.

"What?" said Chantel.

"The magpie rhyme for telling fortunes."

Chantel looked baffled.

Holly chuckled and chanted,

> One for sorrow, two for joy,
> Three for a girl, four for a boy,

Five for silver, six for gold,
Seven for a secret never been told.

Good, that's old magic. Seven for a secret never been told.

Chantel gasped and put a hand up to her head.

The dream horse spoke in words Chantel could understand. Its voice echoed and rolled inside her head. She reeled in the saddle.

Hello, child. Don't be frightened. I'm the White Horse, your friend. Walk towards me.

"Hey?" Holly leaned over and grabbed Snowflake's reins as they slipped from Chantel's fingers. "Are you okay?"

Chantel nodded. The color ebbed and flowed in her cheeks. "Did you hear it?"

"Hear what?"

Only you hear me, child. Do not be afraid. Walk this way.

A sense of warmth and friendship washed over Chantel. She slid off Snowflake and took the reins from Holly. "I'll stop here. You go to the fort. I'll wait. It's cooler here. I'll be okay." She led Snowflake off the track towards a fence across the swell of the hill.

Puzzled, Holly stared after the tiny figure leading the white pony. "How does she know where to go?" she muttered.

Adam and Owen trotted up. Holly pointed. "Look at Chantel. It's as though she's been here before."

Adam gazed resentfully at Chantel. He did not rein in. There was his little sister being "interesting" again! She was always doing something to get attention. She constantly did it to Mom and Dad, and now she was trying it on Holly and

Owen. Well, too bad; this was his holiday and he wanted to see the fort. "She's daydreaming again," he said as he trotted by. "Let her wait. She'll be fine."

Holly and Owen exchanged startled glances.

Chantel looked back and waved happily.

Holly and Owen shrugged. They followed Adam.

The three older children rode to the crest of the hill and dismounted. Holly repeatedly glanced back at Chantel, but the small figure stayed in one spot. Holly turned her attention to Adam and his reaction to seeing the enormous circular ditch and high bank surrounding the flattened summit of the hill.

"I thought you said there was a fort here." Adam was puzzled.

"This is it. This deep ditch and high embankment. It's called Uffington Castle, but it's not a castle made of stone. Up there the bank was topped with a high palisade, a big fence, but the wood rotted away thousands of years ago." Owen pointed into the hollow of the deep ditch. "That was for protection. Dad said there would be stakes sticking out of the bottom, to prevent raids and impale intruders." He grinned, drew an imaginary sword from his belt and started to fight with Adam.

Adam feinted back, slipped and grabbed Owen. They rolled down, over and over until they lay in the ditch bottom, laughing hysterically.

The placid ponies flicked their tails, dropped their heads and lipped the short turf.

"Idiots!" shouted Holly. "Come on. We'll catch it if anyone finds out we've left Chantel on her own."

Adam and Owen scrambled up the sloping sides of the

ditch and dodged around Holly, using her as a shield. Laughing, the three of them led the ponies over to the fence where Chantel had left Snowflake.

Chantel was still standing on the very edge of the hill, staring. Adam, Holly, and Owen joined her.

The view was breathtaking. The hillside dropped away before them, falling steeply towards a wide green valley. But where the short turf began curving downwards, ancient hands had excavated narrow trenches deep into the chalk. The grass had been removed, leaving a series of thick white lines curling over the swell of the hill. The carving was so large that the complete horse could not be seen this close. But the face was clear, a long nose, ears, and a gigantic white eye looking up at the heavens.

"I see you," whispered Chantel. She could feel the magic pulsing from the ground.

Holly, Owen, and Adam were oblivious.

"This smaller side valley is called the Manger." Holly gestured down the steep side of a combe opening onto the main valley. "The White Horse is supposed to feed there at night."

"And see the small conical hill, way down in the middle of it?" Owen pointed.

"The one with no grass on top?" asked Adam.

Owen nodded. "Yup. You'll never guess why."

Adam shook his head.

"That's Dragon Hill. A dragon was killed there. Nothing ever grows where dragon's blood was spilt."

"Cool." Adam stared in fascination at the small, bald-topped hill far below, then turned to join his cousins as they ran beside the chalk lines, tracing the shape and size of the White Horse over the hillside.

Only Chantel stood still, mesmerized by the great white eye at her feet. Slowly she stepped forward and began to walk around it.

Holly turned and saw her. Amazement crossed her face. She stopped and pointed.

"What's up?" Owen asked.

"Did you tell Chantel about walking widdershins around the eye of the White Horse?" asked Holly.

Owen shook his head and also turned to watch.

Adam ran over to them. "What's the matter?"

"It's Chantel." Holly's voice was a breathy whisper. "She's doing the ritual."

Chantel continued to circle the eye.

"She's only walking in circles. She's goofing around again," said Adam.

Holly shook her head. "She's walking widdershins around the eye. If she does it seven times, it's an ancient ritual, a real spell."

Adam looked blank. "Widdershins?"

"Anti-clockwise ... four ... five ... keep counting."

"So what? What's it supposed to do? Turn her into a frog?" Adam laughed.

"'Course not, but she'll get whatever she wishes for in either seven minutes, seven days, seven weeks, seven months, or seven years."

Adam laughed again. "Yeah, right. What are you trying to do? Freak us out?"

Holly laid a hand on his arm. "I'm not trying to freak

anyone out, Adam Maxwell. I'm just telling you what they say in the village. And I hope your little sister has wished wisely, because she has just been round the eye seven times."

Chantel stopped and gazed down at the ancient chalk face. Her dream memory of the beautiful horse was clear and vivid. "I wish I could see you again," she whispered. "I wish you were my horse for the summer."

A roll of thunder rumbled around the valley.

Startled, Holly, Adam, and Owen lifted their faces skyward. Dark blue and purple clouds had built up behind them, rolling, boiling and rapidly obscuring the clear sky.

"Better boogie," shouted Owen. "That's a heck of a storm. Let's get the ponies before they're spooked." He ran uphill towards the fence, Holly following.

Chantel was listening to the voice in her head. She crouched down and scraped frantically at the surface of the chalk eye at her feet.

Adam ran to Chantel, grabbed her arm and tried to pull her away. "Come on, you idiot. We'll be caught in the storm."

Large drops of rain began to splatter the ground.

"You're hurting me." Chantel shook off Adam's grip. She scraped at the chalk again, and plucked something from the ground. It glimmered gold as she closed her palm around it.

"We'll leave you behind," yelled Adam, running uphill. "You'll never find your way back on your own."

"Will so," muttered Chantel as she followed.

The ponies shifted uneasily beside the fence, but quieted when the children arrived. Adam ignored his sister, so Holly helped her mount, then swung up herself.

The rain became a downpour, soaking everyone. The thunder rolled.

"Cut across the hill," called Holly. "It's the short way home. Lean backward as we go downhill. Follow that magpie." She pointed to a lone bird flapping towards the village.

Holly dug her heels into Harlequin's ribs. He snorted and headed across the side of the hill. Adam followed. Chantel held the reins in one hand and clutched the gold in the other. She urged Snowflake forward. Owen brought up the rear.

They were halfway across the slope when it happened.

A spear of lightning sizzled and struck the ground in front of Chantel and Snowflake. A thunderclap shook the earth.

With a whinny of fright Snowflake reared, tossing Chantel like a rag doll. She flew through the air and fell silent and unmoving on the wet grass. Her hand stayed tightly clenched around the gold fragment.

As fast as it had started, the storm stopped.

CHAPTER TWO

TWO FOR JOY

The Wise Ones held council.

Equus's eyes shone. "I've made contact. A girl child sees and hears me."

Myrddin groaned. "One child. Millions of people, but only one child hears us."

Equus stamped a hoof, and a shower of stars sparkled the heavens. "Celebrate, Myrddin! One child is better than none. Besides, three other children were with her. Take heart. Given time perhaps they too will hear us."

"Time is short," snapped Myrddin.

"Shhhh," Ava soothed. "Traa dy liooar, remember. Time enough." She ran a wing down the horse's neck. "Be gentle with the child, Equus. Humans are afraid of powers they do not understand."

Equus hung his head. "I know. I sent a lightning message to them all. But it made her fall, and she broke a leg. She is in a place of healing."

Myrddin tutted and Ava sighed.

"I had forgotten the fragility of human children," Equus said. "But I've sent her healing dreams. She and I will talk again."

"How can you warn a child about the Dark Being?" said Ava sadly.

"I'll explain one task at a time," replied Equus. "She must understand about being a Magic Child before she can help us against the Emptiness."

"We may not have time," Myrddin insisted.

Ava smiled and held out her wings in blessing. "Have faith in the Lady. There will be time enough."

Chantel lay still and white on her hospital bed, her hand still clenched. No one had been able to pry apart her fingers.

Only the occasional flicker of her closed eyelids showed she was alive. But though she seemed unconscious, she spoke with the White Horse.

Hello, child.

Is that you, Horse? Did my wish come true? Are you my horse now?

Yes, I'm the Great White Horse, and you are the Magic Child.

What does that mean?

That together you and I can ride the wind and share

*magical secrets. Relax. Open your heart and mind to me.
You are the new Magic Child with a powerful gift. But now
you must heal, so sleep and dream, sleep and dream. You
can learn through your dreams. Dream of the past, child.
See through the eyes of Alin, one of the people you call
Celts. He was the first Magic Child.*

⊠ ⊠ ⊠

Alin stood among the circle of youths on the hilltop. Many
were hopeful, some were apprehensive, and one or two shook
with terror.

Not Alin. He stood proud and straight. This was the day
he had prepared for all his fourteen summers on earth. The
Day of the King, the day the Celtic people honored the
Great White Horse God, the day the Chosen One would
ride the wind like the Horse God himself.

Alin pulled back his shoulders and stood tall in the sunshine, a tiny smile on his lips. He watched intently. His
heart knew his fate.

The hooded body of the oldest priest spun blindly in
the center of the circle, faster and faster, dizzily swinging his
staff in front of the boys. Finally, the priest staggered to a
stop, just as Alin knew he would, with the staff pointing
unerringly at him.

The other boys gave a whispering sigh as they drew back,
leaving Alin alone. He strode towards the edge of the hillside.
The crowds gathered on the terraces far below in the valley
known as the Manger saw that a choice had been made. A
faint roar of approving voices drifted upward on the wind.

Alin eyed the tabooed slope down to the Manger. It was a long way down and heart-stoppingly steep, but this moment was what he had secretly trained for. He could ride it — given the right horse.

Next Alin turned towards Dragon Hill.

There stood the distant, glittering, gold-clad figure of the current king. Alin raised his arm in salute and bowed. The tiny figure raised its arm in acknowledgement.

Stepping back from the edge, Alin turned and looked at the hooded priest. The priest's staff gestured towards the horse corral built on the crest of the hill between the carved chalk spine of the Great White Horse and the protective ditch circling the hilltop fort.

Alin looked over the wattle fence and surveyed this year's choices. They were fine horses, strong and wiry, their muscles playing under their haunches as they nervously moved around the small space. His eye lit on a red mare with a foal nuzzling anxiously against her side. The mare turned her head and gazed unblinkingly at Alin. As their eyes met, Alin's heart quickened. She could do it. She had the wiriness and sure-footedness to tackle the hill, the strength in her hindquarters to hold on, and the will to survive for her foal. He stretched out his hand and exhaled gently.

The mare's ears flickered and she stepped forward and let him rub her forehead.

Two more priests appeared. One grasped the mare's forelock, threw the gold and enameled bridle over her head and buckled the small ceremonial saddle with gold stirrups onto her back. The other took Alin's arm. He was led away, back to the edge of the hill, where he was rapidly stripped and left to stand naked and vulnerable.

All this was done in silence save for the wind, the rustle of dry grass, the occasional whicker from the horses, and the ethereal song of the skylark.

Alin drew a deep breath, spicy with earthy smells, the sweat of horses and humans, the dusty chalk, the smoky odor of the priest's wool and leather robes, and the acrid smell of fear from several of the youths in the surrounding semi-circle. He glanced back at them, aware that now he was no longer part of their easygoing group. He was no longer a fellow conspirator in a prank against the elders, a worthy opponent on the wrestling ground, or a trusted partner in the wild boar hunt. Now he was the Chosen One. The few yards between him and his comrades were as great a distance as that between them and the far horizon.

Alin glanced at each well-known face. Some reflected awe, others pity and grief, some fear, and several gazed back as though he were a stranger. Only his best friend Halydd shared his joy. They exchanged a glance of triumph as the priests chanted a blessing and the attending acolytes responded with their ritual keening.

Once again the old priest raised his staff. The mare was led forward. The people roared, and Alin knew his time had come.

The old priest threw back his hood and lifted a braided necklace of white horse hair from around his neck. A gold talisman twisted and twinkled in the sunlight. He threw the necklace over Alin's head.

Alin glanced down. The outline of the White Horse was etched into the golden circle. He clasped the talisman and held it to his heart. "May the Great White Horse God be with me," he murmured, and dropped the braid against his chest as he turned to his horse.

Grasping the bridle, Alin knotted it loosely and looped it over his arm. Next he twisted his bridle hand into the red mare's mane. "I won't drag on your mouth, little mare," he whispered in her ear. "I'll stick to your back like a burr." He leapt into the saddle. Using his knees he urged the mare forward towards the very edge of the steep slope into the Manger.

The crowd below roared again, then fell silent.

As he looked again down the almost vertical drop, Alin's stomach cramped with fear. He felt the red mare's answering shudder of terror as she realized what was demanded of her. There was no going back ... his fate was sealed. He was the Chosen One. Death was ahead of him, either within the next seven minutes or at the end of the next seven years. It had always been so for the Chosen Ones.

Alin's terrified gaze flickered towards the golden king far below on top of the dragon mound. He knew for the first time the terrible glory of being the Chosen One. Seven years ago the king had been a youth like him, and now his fate rested on Alin's skill. Alin trembled. Blackness began to gather behind his eyes.

Just then Halydd started to sing.

Come all ye men at arms,
Choose your horse, and sing.

Strong and true, Halydd's voice rang out.

We'll leap the downs, and ride the wind,
And glorify the king.

One by one the other boys joined in. Defiantly they roared the chorus together.

We'll glorify the king.
We'll glorify the king.
We'll leap the downs, and ride the wind,
And glorify the king.

Alin's heart lifted and the blackness receded. His friends in arms were with him again, egging him on to ride the wind. This was what it was all for — to glorify the Horse King — to perform a great feat that would show the Horse King that his followers were worthy of protection for another seven years.

Alin gave a great yell, "To the Horse King!" and jabbed his heels hard into the ribs of the red mare.

She leapt forward over the edge and began the heart-stopping downward journey.

A piercing whinny came from the horse corral as the foal realized her mother had gone. The small creature took the wattle fence at a standing leap, scattered the priests and followed.

Astounded, youths, priests, king, and spectators watched the foal leap over the edge and slip and slither in the wake of Alin and the red mare's death-defying descent. In a trance, Alin felt the world pass by in slow motion. He closed his eyes and concentrated on keeping his balance and helping the red mare ride the wind.

The wind roared in his ears, competing with the blood pounding in his head and his heart's rapid beats. Alin heard the red mare's frantic scrabbles and hoof beats as she struggled against the vertical pull of gravity forcing the pace. He gripped with his thighs, thrusting his heels forward over her withers, and lay right back against her haunches to compensate for his weight. His body was one with hers. He willed her to fly.

A great gasp came from the crowd below as the miracle occurred.

The wind seemed to cradle the boy, mare, and foal, gently bouncing them from tussock to tussock in great graceful leaps. All three flew downwards at one with the spirit of the Great White Horse. Only once did the mare's haunches start to slip to one side, but her hind muscles bunched and she dug in her hooves. Alin shifted his weight and felt her right herself during the next leap.

This was riding. This was how the Great White Horse galloped from hilltop to hilltop. This heart-stopping, breathtaking descent was truly riding the wind.

Neither of them heard the roar of the crowd as they reached the bottom, the foal still scrambling in their wake. Alin became aware that the angle of the descent had changed. He rapidly changed position until he was crouched low over the red mare's neck. Together they galloped the full length of the valley to stop trembling and dripping with sweat and lather beneath the Blessed Thorn. The foal arrived a few seconds later and stuck like glue to its mother's flank and Alin's leg.

Startled, two magpies fluttered up from the branches,

calling joyously. Alin threw back his head and laughed with relief. Two for joy — the omens were certainly with him today.

The Blowing Stone's deep note echoed around the valley. Dimly, Alin realized it was being sounded in respect for the previous king. He gently nudged the red mare and foal. All three looked towards Dragon Hill.

The young king spread his arms wide in joyful acceptance of the knife stroke that would unite him forever with the Great White Horse God. As the king's body dropped, Alin slid from the red mare's back and fell to his knees in a gesture of honor. For the next seven years he would be keeper of the White Horse and king to his people.

He rose, patted the red mare's flank and ran a comforting hand over the back of the trembling foal. Two horses had ridden the wind. Two for joy! What a powerful omen! A strong omen that the priests could only interpret as good. He, Alin, would honor these horses in a special way so that they would always be linked with him and his reign. He would have their image carved on a hillside. Yes, into the red clay beyond the downs. A carving like that of the Great White Horse God, one big enough to be seen from afar. Yes, that's what he would do. He would show his thanks by offering his brave red mare and her foal to the White Horse God as a fitting tribute.

His eye lit upon a small sharp stone. He bent down and picked it up. Using the sharp point, he swiftly scratched a second horse into the gold talisman. Then he held it up towards the carving on the hill. His voice rang out, "Thank you, Great White Horse God. You sent me power and blessing. In return I will give you a mate."

Alin tossed the stone and dropped the talisman back around his neck. It winked in the sunlight. Then he proudly walked back up the valley to meet his new subjects and to accept the golden cloak from the high priest.

The red mare and foal followed.

All that happened a long time ago?

Yes, child.

You are the Horse King?

Yes, child. That is one of my names.

Chantel's body shivered with awe. *And Alin was the Magic Child?*

He was the first.

Then how can I help you? I'm not brave like Alin. I'm just a kid.

You can help. You have a special power. A belief in dreams and imagination. Humans call it intuition. I need that power to help find the red mare and foal that Alin created. They have disappeared from the memory of your people and your world is so changed I can no longer see where they lie. They were my mate and child. I miss them. Equus sighed. *Will you help them ride the wind with me again?*

How? ... I don't understand. Chantel's unconscious body showed her distress. She tossed and turned restlessly on the hospital bed.

The old magic is almost forgotten, but you can help renew it. Talk with the other young people. If everyone helps, we will find the red mare and the old magic will be strengthened. Magic still lives if there are believers.

Am I a believer?

You are. You performed the ritual.

But how can I make the others believe?

Remember what you found at my carving? Part of my magic talisman is still clasped in your hand. Ask the others to take it to Wayland's Smithy.

Wayland's Smithy, Chantel repeated slowly. She turned in her sleep and her free hand touched the closed fist. Her fingers visibly tightened again.

Yes, I'll help you, White Horse. Chantel's lips curved into a faint smile and her body relaxed on the bed. She murmured the strange name "Wayland's Smithy" aloud, slipped her fist under her pillow and drifted into a deep, natural sleep.

⬚ ⬚ ⬚

The doctor who had been leaning over Chantel's bed straightened and turned to her Auntie Lynne and Uncle Ron.

"She'll do. She's out of the anesthetic and sleeping naturally. She'll drift in and out of sleep for a couple of days. But then she should be fine. We'll keep her under observation until she is fully alert. But I have every confidence you'll be able to take her home on Wednesday." He patted the cast on Chantel's leg and turned to go.

Chantel shifted in her bed and muttered, "Wayland's Smithy," but her eyes did not open.

Her aunt and uncle leaned closer to catch what she said.

"Ignore anything she mutters. She's dreaming." The doctor smiled at Uncle Ron and Auntie Lynne. "Concussion sometimes temporarily affects the mind. She might wake up confused, or have vivid dreams she thinks are real. It's quite normal. It will pass."

※ ※ ※

Adam, Owen, and Holly sat by the telephone.

Adam seemed to have shrunk. His eyes looked enormous, and his red hair and freckles stood out against his white face. He shivered and pulled a worn traveling blanket further around his shoulders.

"Mum says shock makes you feel cold," Holly said.

Adam tugged the blanket angrily. "I hope Chantel's not badly hurt. Mom and Dad will be mad. I was supposed to look after her. They'll say it was my fault, just you watch. I knew there would be trouble if Chantel came to England with me. Things always happen to her, then get blamed on me."

"Don't be daft," Owen said. "You didn't cause the lightning. No one's going to blame you. We're all lucky to be alive."

BRIIIINNG-BRIIINNNG. BRIIIINNG-BRIIINNNG.

Three hands shot towards the telephone, but Owen reached it first.

"Uffington 6291, Owen speaking."

"Hello, son. Tell everyone Chantel is going to be okay."

"Hold on, Dad. I'll put you on the speaker."

Owen pressed a switch and Uncle Ron's voice filled the room. "Chantel has a concussion and a broken leg."

Adam gasped. "How bad is it, Uncle Ron?"

"She'll be fine. The break was clean. She can have the plaster off in six weeks."

Everyone groaned.

"That's the summer gone. Poor kid," whispered Holly.

"The doctors checked the concussion," continued Uncle Ron. "She's fine but needs rest and quiet in hospital for a couple of days. Then she can come home and recuperate at the farm."

"Can we visit her?" asked Adam shakily.

"Not today. She's still groggy from the anesthetic. You can visit tomorrow afternoon. She keeps on muttering about her white horse. You can reassure her about Snowflake."

"Okay," said Adam quietly.

Uncle Ron's voice softened. "Don't worry, Adam. Chantel will recover. She's lucky. You all are. A lightning strike so close but no one hit. It's a miracle.

"By the way, Adam, I've phoned your folks and left a message. It's about three AM in Canada, but I'm sure they'll be in contact when they wake up. We're coming home soon. Everything all right there?"

"We were just worried," Holly said. "It took ages for you to phone."

"I know. We waited until Chantel came round from the anesthetic. Once she spoke, we knew she was fine. You can stop worrying now, promise?"

"Promise," everyone called back, grinning shakily at each other.

"How are the ponies?" Uncle Ron asked.

"Mr. O'Reilly has seen to them," Owen said. "He's rubbed them down and settled them in the barn. And Mrs. O'Reilly gave us tea, but Adam's not eaten much."

"Adam. You're not to worry about Chantel. Understand?"

"Yes, Uncle Ron."

"Auntie Lynne and I will be home soon. Hang in there."

With a loud click Uncle Ron rang off, leaving the speaker buzzing until Owen leaned over and switched it off.

The cousins looked at each other.

"I was scared Chantel would die." Holly voiced everyone's fears.

Adam nodded, his throat too tight to speak.

"Poor kid — that broken leg will spoil her holiday. We must find ways to make it up to her," said Owen.

"What about the old pony carriage in the back of the barn?" said Holly. "If we clean it up we can take her out in it. Then she won't miss out on our trips."

"Great idea." Owen thumped his sister's arm affectionately. "We'll make sure the holiday isn't ruined."

They both grinned at Adam.

CHAPTER THREE

THE BROKEN TALISMAN

Holly, Owen, and Adam walked towards the hospital room, wondering what they would find.

"Chantel Maxwell? She's in there," said the nurse, pointing out the doorway. "She needs rest. Don't stay long, and don't excite or upset her."

Chantel lay against her pillows, half-dozing. A large hump under the bedclothes marked the wire cage protecting her plastered leg. She looked small in the big bed.

Adam's heart twinged with pity.

Hearing footsteps in the doorway, Chantel turned her head. Her face was pale and there were deep circles under her eyes. Her smile was anxious. "You're here at last." Her voice was soft but urgent. Her eyes checked behind them. "Good, no grown-ups! I need to talk to you ... about the White Horse."

"Snowflake's fine." Adam bent over and gave her a clumsy hug. "All the ponies are."

Holly and Owen nodded their agreement.

"No ... no ... not Snowflake." Chantel pushed Adam away and struggled to sit. "The real White Horse. The one carved in the hill." She dropped her voice. "He's real. He talks to me."

Adam and her cousins avoided her eyes.

There was a long pause.

Adam cleared his throat and spoke gruffly. "You've been er ... dreaming, Chantel. It's ... it's ... the bump on your head."

Holly nodded. "Yes ... that's right. The doctor said concussion does weird things," she added kindly.

Chantel's eyes filled with tears. "You don't believe me. I knew you wouldn't." She rolled away from them, pulling the pillow over her face.

A small object fell to the floor with a faint tinkle.

"You've dropped something." Holly bent down and picked up a flat golden shape. She held it up.

Chantel turned back, uncovered one eye and glared, then realized what Holly was showing her. She pulled down the pillow and leaned up on her elbow. "I forgot it was under my pillow ... Now you have to believe me. The horse said to give it to you."

"What is it?" Holly peered at it. "Where did you get it?" She passed it over to Owen. He and Adam examined it.

"It looks like half an old coin, a real gold coin," said Owen. "Who gave it you?"

They all looked at Chantel.

She flushed. "You won't believe me." Her voice sharpened

defiantly. "I got it from the White Horse. It's not a coin. It's a talisman."

"There are marks on it," said Adam. He plucked the gold object from Owen's hand and carried it over to the window where the light was brighter. He turned it several times. "One side is kind of like a whorl, but the other side reminds me of ..." Adam's voice was unsure. He held out the talisman on the palm of his hand so that Owen and Holly could look. "... part of the horse carving on the hill."

The three kids stared down at the broken gold piece and looked uneasily back at Chantel.

Adam laughed. "The horse didn't give this to you. You're lying. You found it! You were digging in the chalk just before the storm. I saw you!"

Chantel's eyes filled with tears, but she brushed them away with her fist. "Yes, I found it in the eye ... But the White Horse told me to do it. He did give me the talisman, Adam Maxwell. He did! He's asked me to help him, and he needs your help too. And that's proof! You're supposed to take it to somewhere. But I told him you wouldn't believe me."

"Yeah, right!" Adam snorted.

Holly kicked Adam's ankle to shut him up. She patted Chantel's arm.

Chantel turned to Holly. "I'm telling the truth. Honestly! The talisman has to go to ... " Her brow furrowed as she tried to remember the strange name. "To Why ... land ... Smith something."

"Smithy?" asked Holly in an odd voice "Wayland's Smithy?"

"Yes," said Chantel, her face clearing. "That's right."

34

Holly and Owen looked at each other. There was a long silence.

"Weird," said Owen finally. He shook his head slowly. "Totally weird. How did you come up with that?"

"I told you. The White Horse told me. Take the talisman to Wayland's Smithy. You'll see."

"See what?" asked Owen.

Chantel gave a small shrug. "Dunno. He didn't say. But I bet something will happen to make you believe me," she finished.

"I don't get it, you guys. What's going on?" Adam interrupted the three-way conversation.

"We're not sure," said Holly. "But somehow your little sister has learned about Wayland's Smithy. It's a historic site, an old barrow along the Ridgeway. An ancient burial place."

"I thought a smithy was another name for a blacksmith shop," said Adam.

"It is. That's part of the story. Wayland's Smithy is the oldest prehistoric site in the area. It's a long, grass-covered burial mound supposedly built by a god called Wayland, who was a blacksmith. The story says if a traveler leaves a horse there overnight, and places a silver coin on the rock at the barrow entrance, the horse will be magically shod by morning. So that's why the barrow's called a smithy," Owen explained. "Come on, Chantel ... who told you about it?"

Chantel glared at them. "The White Horse," she said.

There was an awkward silence.

Chantel's voice shook. "Okay, fine. Don't believe me ... I don't want to talk anymore. Go away!" She turned over and pretended to sleep, but a tear trickled from the corner of her eye.

※ ※ ※

Adam, Owen, and Holly retreated in disarray down the hospital corridor and stood in a huddle by an elevator.

"We weren't supposed to upset her," Holly said.

"I know," Owen agreed. "Mum said the concussion might make her hallucinate. But what are we supposed to do? Go along with everything?"

Adam shrugged.

Holly tried to grapple with the problem. "You know her best, Adam. Does Chantel honestly believe the White Horse is real?"

Adam turned the gold fragment over and over in his hand. "She's always making things up," he muttered crossly. "She does it to get attention." Then honesty got the better of him. "But she seemed serious this time."

"Yeah, but is she seriously nuts with concussion, or ..." Owen trailed off.

"Or is this from the White Horse?" Adam finished. "Come on, you guys. How could it be?" He tossed the talisman into the air. They watched as it spun back into his hand.

"I dunno," Owen said slowly. "But where did she get it? There are weird stories in our village. People are always talking about horse magic. What if she *is* telling the truth? What if it's the spell?"

Adam rolled his eyes towards Holly, thinking she'd back him up.

"Yes, yes. I forgot!" Holly's voice rose in excitement.

"Chantel walked widdershins seven times around the eye. I bet I know what she wished for. I bet she wanted to see the real White Horse."

Owen's eyes widened. "And ... and ... the villagers say you get your wish in units of seven." His voice quickened. "It was about seven minutes later the storm started and the lightning struck!"

"And ever since she says she's been talking to the White Horse," Holly finished.

"She could dream up the horse, but how could she dream up the talisman and Wayland's Smithy?" added Owen.

"Exactly!" Holly finished.

"Hey, hold it. What are you two saying?" Adam interrupted.

Holly shrugged. "I suppose we're saying we might owe Chantel an apology. Maybe we should go back and really listen to what she has to say."

Adam stared at them in disbelief. "You're joking!"

"What have we got to lose?" asked Owen. "She's either hallucinating, in which case we go along with it for now and all have a good laugh when she gets better, or her stories are true and we're in for an adventure!"

Adam snorted with angry laughter. Owen was supposed to be doing things with him, and now his little sister was sidetracking things. "You're nuts. If you believe that, you'll believe anything."

"Okay, we're nuts." Owen pushed Adam up the corridor by the small of his back. "Go and talk to Chantel. You're her brother."

Adam twisted away. "No way. You believe that rubbish, you talk to her."

"Oh, shut up, you two. I'll go." Holly retraced her steps to Chantel's room, leaving the two boys glaring at each other.

⊠ ⊠ ⊠

"Chantel, can I come in?"

Holly poked her head around the door.

Chantel turned a tear-streaked face towards her. She gave a little nod.

"We didn't mean to upset you." Holly perched on the foot of the bed. "But it's pretty weird."

Chantel blew her nose noisily. "You think it's weird? You're not the one hearing the horse." She gave a hiccup. "It's more than just hitting my head."

Holly leaned forward and dropped her voice. "I think it's because you did a spell."

"I did? What spell?" asked Chantel.

Holly chose her words with care. " Do you remember walking around the eye of the White Horse?"

Chantel nodded, her eyes wary.

"Why did you do it?"

Chantel said nothing, but her fingers played with the bedsheet.

Holly patted her leg. "Come on ... tell me, Chantel. I promise not to think you're nuts."

"Promise," Chantel whispered.

"I promise."

"I heard the White Horse in my head. He told me what to do."

"And what did you do?" Holly prompted.

"I ... I walked around the eye ... seven times ... and made a wish."

Holly caught her breath. "So I was right. Did you wish for the White Horse?"

Chantel's voice shook. "H ... how did you know?"

"I figured it out. I know a bit about horse magic." Holly grinned. "It's so weird it must be true. Can the others come in? Will you tell us everything?"

"Okay." Chantel sat up and looked more cheerful.

Holly went to the doorway and waved in Adam and Owen.

"Sorry, Chantel." Owen tried to look contrite, but his eyes danced.

Chantel grinned shakily back.

Adam hesitated at the door, then perched uneasily on the end of the bed beside Holly.

Owen grabbed the chair, turned it back to front and straddled it. "So, tell us the lot. Right from the beginning."

"From the very beginning?" asked Chantel.

"Yes," chorused everyone.

"Then I guess it all started the night we arrived from Canada."

"It did?" said Holly.

"Yes, you were all asleep," said Chantel. "And I saw a shooting star ..."

She told the whole story.

"Amazing," said Owen.

"So I've promised to help him," Chantel finished. "I've said I'll help the White Horse find the red horse that Alin made." She lay back on her pillow, her eyelids drooping.

"I can't imagine anyone riding down the Manger like Alin did," said Owen. "And I can't imagine how you could have made it up," he finished. "Not unless you've read a book or seen a TV show about the early Celts."

Chantel shook her head. "Nope. I only know what the White Horse showed me." She closed her eyes.

Holly stood up. "Come on. Chantel's exhausted and we weren't supposed to tire her." She leaned over and kissed Chantel's cheek. "You rest. We'll check out some stuff for you."

Chantel's eyes flew open again. "You will?"

Holly nodded. "We'll ask around. See what we can find out about the history of the White Horse and if anyone has ever heard of a red horse as part of the story."

Adam, his hands stuck deep in his pockets, slumped against the bottom of the bed. He gazed with bemusement and frustration at his little sister. She'd done it again! She'd made up a wonderful story that had held everyone entranced. She was always doing it. A wave of anger swept through him. His parents loved Chantel's stories, but if he made anything up they called him a liar! His fingers suddenly touched the hard edge of the talisman. His hand closed over the one tiny piece of reality in the whole incredible story.

Huh, thought Adam. She's not going to be able to lie about this for long. He drew his hand out of his pocket and held the talisman in the air. "So? What about this?" he said.

"We'll take it to Wayland's Smithy tomorrow morning," said Holly. "See if anything happens."

CHAPTER FOUR

THREE FOR A GIRL

Moonlight drifted through the cracks in the hospital blinds and banded Chantel's bed. Chantel had slept soundly all late afternoon and evening, relieved that Adam, Holly, and Owen had finally believed her. Now she was wide awake and worrying.

She lifted her head and squinted at the clock on the wall. It was just after midnight. She slumped back on the pillow. Her head throbbed, her leg itched inside the cast, and she was scared.

What if Adam was right and the lightning had fried her brain? What if she was going mad?

Her eyes wandered around the hospital room. She'd sent her brother and cousins to Wayland's Smithy. What if nothing happened? They'd tell the doctors and nurses she was crazy and she'd be stuck in hospital forever.

She sighed.

A feeling of warmth and friendship washed over her with the moonlight.

"Is that you, Horse? Are you there?" Chantel whispered into the darkness.

I'm always here.

I can't sleep. I'm scared. I wish we could go riding, Chantel said, silently this time.

The White Horse whickered softly. *We can. It's time for me to show you Alin's red mare.*

Chantel felt herself rise upward.

Couldn't be! She was sitting astride the White Horse, floating high in the starlit sky. Terrified, she closed her eyes, wound her fingers into the silky mane and clung like a monkey to the broad back.

Relax. You are the Magic Child. You won't fall.

Chantel opened one eye and squinted down again.

The sleeping earth lay far below, its horizon curving gently. The city gleamed with strings of streetlights, glittering windows, and dancing trails of light from moving cars. She could even pick out the hospital. Beyond the city the countryside was cloaked in velvet darkness with only a sparkle here and there.

It's beautiful. Chantel opened both eyes, sat up and gazed with wonder. Around her the stars danced.

The White Horse softly blew through his nostrils. *It's always beautiful. Each time I ride the wind I see changes. But it's always beautiful.*

They were off. In one bound the city was gone, and they leapt to the crest of the downs. Chantel recognized the village of Uffington and her cousins' farmhouse. Then they were above the White Horse carving, with the Manger and Dragon Hill lying far below.

What happened to the red mare? asked Chantel eagerly inside her mind. *Did Alin carve her likeness on the hill?*

Yes. Alin created more horse magic and for over two thousand years the red mare and her foal ran with me. I'll show you how fine she looked at the time of a powerful king's reign. King Alfred the Great recognized the importance of old magic, but his bishop did not.

Watch carefully. We will neither be seen nor heard.

The White Horse leapt across the valley and into the past. Chantel gasped. The night sky changed to a glorious sunset as they landed on a hilltop. A straggle of men clad in Saxon tunics walked past them.

❈ ❈ ❈

King Alfred followed the lithe shepherd boy over the brow of the hill. His men stumbled wearily after them. Egbert, his chief advisor, lurched suddenly and cursed under his breath.

Alfred shot out an arm to steady him.

"Grateful thanks, my liege. I missed noting a rabbit hole. The fading light is deceptive."

Alfred grinned. "I should arrange future marches only in broad daylight, eh?"

Egbert chuckled. "Aye, and across flat meadows, with an inn and good ale at the end of each day." The men guffawed.

The evening was warm. They reached the top. Alfred motioned his company to rest. He wiped the sweat from his face.

His men loosened their woolen tunics to catch the fitful breeze. They gazed with surprise across the valley. On the opposite hillside was a carving. Between patches of woodland, a large grassy slope showed off deep lines carved into red clay. A red horse with a white eye was slashed into the turf. A smaller horse was carved running beside it. The pair glowed in the golden rays of the setting sun and looked ready to gallop off across the hillside.

Alfred's heart sang. This was the art of his people. He was almost home. "I've not seen the red mare for many a year. 'Tis an impressive sight, is it not?" he said.

"Impressive indeed, sire. But I was told the great horse carving was in white chalk." Egbert looked to the king.

"'Tis so, Egbert. Yonder is a different carving done by the same ancient people."

"Aye. There be the Vale of the Red Horse." The shepherd boy pointed to a collection of wattle and daub huts at the base of the hill. "Your pallet be here for the night. I reckon you be reaching White Horse Vale day after the morrow. 'Tis a two-day march from here."

Alfred looked at the tumbledown hovels and sighed. He feasted his eyes on the glowing carving as he walked downhill. "'Tis skillfully made, is it not? The white eye makes it live."

"Is the eye made of marble?" Egbert asked as he followed.

The shepherd boy laughed. "Nay, nobbut red soil and yellow rock round here. Yonder eye be a bucketful of chalk carried from White Horse Vale every seven years."

The voices faded as the small company moved away.

Did the chalk come from you? wondered Chantel.

The White Horse nodded. *Alin linked us forever. Chalk from my eye is placed in the red mare's eye. Come, we must follow King Alfred.*

The horse soared off the hilltop and landed in the valley by the open door of a tumbledown hut. Chantel leaned to one side to peek in.

▨ ▨ ▨

Alfred and Egbert sat before a small fire in the middle of the floor. Without his sword and helmet, Alfred was shown to be a young man of some twenty-three summers. His advisor was not much older. Alfred removed a wooden skewer of roasting rabbit from the coals and tore the meat in half. He tossed a portion to Egbert and sucked his singed fingers.

Egbert grinned and speared the half-raw meat with his dagger. He held it over the coals again. "You have many talents, sire, but cooking is not one of them," he remarked.

Alfred ignored him. He gnawed at the meat while gazing into the flames. "Egbert, I am baffled. These hills are my homelands. My mother bore me in White Horse Vale. Yet the people here and in all the hidden valleys between this place and the Vale of the White Horse know me as their king, yet know me not!"

Egbert nodded. "They have heard you are their king. But this means nothing to them. These places are distant from your palace at Winchester. Until now, only the traveling bards bring news of you." He shrugged. "And if the Dane force strikes, what good is a king from the vales who is out of reach?"

"You speak wisdom. We must make my presence real. I must find a way to command allegiance." Alfred fell silent.

Egbert stirred. "These horses carved upon the hills. Are they worshiped, sire? Do vale people not follow the teachings of St. Augustine?"

Alfred shrugged. "'Tis hard to tell. The monks built a small monastery nearby, and a bigger one in Wantage, the town where I was born. The people worship on Sundays and Saint days, but still revere the Great White Horse."

He gazed into the flames, then looked up, his eyes bright. "I have it, Egbert. I will bring the horse symbol of the vale people together with the trappings of my kingship. We will ask the blessings of the True Faith and choose a girl child and boy child from the area to be part of the ceremony. In a sennight's time I will be crowned on White Horse Hill."

Egbert clapped his hands together.

Alfred held up his palm to show he had not finished. "And I will decree a palace be built in Wantage, the most important town in White Horse Vale."

"Masterly, sire," Egbert approved. "Masterly."

❈ ❈ ❈

"Ooooh, can we watch the coronation?" whispered Chantel aloud into the ear of the White Horse. "I've always wanted to see a king or queen crowned."

We can. It's an important part of the story. Watch for the Magic Child. Equus leapt over the hills, through space and time, to land on the earthworks of Uffington Castle on White Horse Hill.

The hill was crowded with people.

Bustling camps housed people from afar. The local folk walked up from Uffington. The old were carried in litters and babies carried in arms. The air was alive with songs and stories.

Alfred's men helped each group to cross the ditch, enter the earthworks and choose a place to watch from the top of the great embankments circling the flat plateau.

Finally the thousands were so closely seated that not a blade of grass could be seen.

A distant fanfare of trumpets sounded.

Heads turned towards the entrance. Mounted soldiers, purple-edged cloaks flying, burst through the gap and circled the plateau several times at great speed. Then, in a flurry of dust, they reined in their horses and stood around the edge.

The trumpets rang out again, much closer this time.

A small boy carrying a staff topped with a gleaming gold cross solemnly stepped through the entrance. Behind him walked the Bishop of Wantage and his monks. The bishop led them to the center of the grass, and the monks formed a horseshoe around him.

Two heralds appeared and raised trumpets to their lips. A volley of notes rent the air. A horse whinnied.

With a collective gasp, the entire crowd rose to its feet, roaring its approval.

Alfred had appeared, mounted on a white horse whose ancient bridle and stirrups were finely enameled gold. He was clothed in an unadorned tunic of the royal purple. His fair head was bare. His youthful countenance glowed.

The king held a leading rein. On the end stepped a red mare, a foal hugging her side. Astride the red mare's back sat a girl of seven summers. She wore a white shift with a gold talisman hanging from a thin braid around her neck. Proudly she held aloft a branch from the sacred thorn tree. On it hung a shining gold band.

⊠ ⊠ ⊠

Horse, is she the Magic Child?
Yes. That's Ethrelda.

⊠ ⊠ ⊠

Alfred dismounted, bowed first to the bishop, then to the people. The crowd roared once more and seated themselves. Alfred walked across the grass to the bishop and knelt humbly before him.

The bishop turned and motioned briskly to the child with the sacred thorn branch. Ethrelda slid off the red mare, stepped forward and offered him the branch. The bishop removed the plain gold circlet.

He lifted it in the air for all to see, made the sign of the cross over it and placed it on Alfred's brow. The monks bowed their heads and intoned a prayer in Latin. The words were unknown to the people, but after a moment a scatter of "amens" rolled around the crowd.

The bishop held out his hand, helped Alfred to his feet, turned him and presented him to the multitude as the monks softly chanted.

"Your king, Alfred the Great," the bishop shouted.

The people watched and waited respectfully.

Suddenly a clear high voice was heard. "Glorify the king," shouted little Ethrelda.

"Glorify the king," a woman's voice joined in from the crowd.

"Yes, glorify the king," called an old man.

The shout was taken up throughout the crowd.

Alfred and his entourage beamed. The bishop and his monks looked startled.

Ethrelda began to sing the ancient song.

> We'll glorify the king
> We'll glorify the king.

The crowd joined in.

> We'll leap the downs, and ride the wind,
> And glorify the king.

As the people sang, Ethrelda slipped past the dignitaries, removing her necklace on the way. She thrust the gold talisman on its horse-hair braid into Alfred's hand and indicated that he should hang it around his neck.

Smiling, Alfred did so.

Ethrelda darted towards the large rock standing at one side of the circle. The bishop whispered to a monk to stop her, but she slipped past the outstretched hands.

Taking a deep breath, Ethrelda bent over a hole in the rock and blew as hard as she could. A great booming sound rolled around the enclosure. Three magpies rose chattering from the ditch and circled overhead. Ethrelda looked up at the circling birds, noted their number and blew again. The sound rolled over White Horse Hill. Once more she blew, and the gigantic voice of the ceremonial Blowing Stone spilled over the downs and into the vale.

A mighty cheer went up.

Alfred and Egbert exchanged glances of delight.

"You did it, sire," whispered Egbert. "The people are with you." He nudged Alfred. "But look at the bishop's face. He is angry."

"That I can repair," Alfred whispered back.

The tumult died down. Alfred stepped forward to speak. He motioned for the bishop to join him.

"I humbly thank you all." His gesture included everyone. "To mark this coronation I ask the bishop to accept a gift from me." He placed a soft leather purse filled with gold in the bishop's hand. "This gold is for you, good bishop, to further your work bringing the glory of God to these vales."

Delight fought the disapproval on the bishop's face. He swiftly stowed the purse in the pocket of his voluminous robes, bowed low over Alfred's hand and kissed his ring in a gesture of allegiance. "Thank you, Your Majesty." His voice dropped to a hissing whisper. "But, I pray you, remove that heathen object from around your neck."

"Later, bishop, later," replied Alfred softly. He touched the talisman. "A token from the people does no harm."

The bishop retreated, an angry flush staining his neck.

Alfred turned once again to the people.

"Men of the vales," he called. "Will you help me raise a palace in Wantage? A place to which my men and I can come to prevent the forays from the Danelaw threatening these peaceful valleys?"

"Aye!" roared a thousand voices. "We will help."

"Then 'tis as good as done," said Alfred. He surveyed the crowd. "Tell me, good folks, if what I once knew remains true. Every seventh summer, do the people of these vales still scour clean the white and red horses on the hills?"

"We do," the crowd called back.

Alfred produced a second purse, waved it in the air for all to see and dropped it in the bishop's hand.

"Then I charge the bishop to use this gold to provide food and drink to the scourers of future years, in memory of this day." Alfred waved towards the entrance. Soldiers appeared. They carried skins full of mead into the circle. Women followed, dragging great baskets of bread.

"My people — I invite you to break bread with me." Alfred took a loaf, broke it in two and offered it to the crowd.

The cheering could be heard for miles.

After the meal, Alfred led the dignitaries from the earthworks.

❈ ❈ ❈

We must follow, said the White Horse. He passed through the crowd and paused outside the embankment where Alfred and the coronation retinue had gathered.

❈ ❈ ❈

Alfred nodded graciously to the bishop. "'Twas well done. Thank you, bishop."

The bishop bowed. "I had hoped not to include reference to the horse and the stone. I pray you, sire, now you are beyond the gaze of the peasants, remove the heathen horse emblem."

Shocked, Ethrelda gazed from bishop to king.

The king fingered the talisman. "'Tis a pretty piece, and far older than the kings of England if the stories be true. Mayhap the kingship should keep it safe."

The bishop lost his temper. His hand shot out and snatched the horse-hair braid. The ancient strands parted and the talisman dropped to the ground. The bishop smote the talisman with his staff. The soft gold broke in two. "'Tis blasphemy, sire. Have an end to it! As king you must uphold the teachings of St. Augustine and the One True Faith."

The king's men leapt forward, swords drawn.

Alfred raised his arm and stopped them. He looked at the bishop through narrowed eyes "Take care your role be not overstepped, bishop. Watch over the spiritual health of the people, but leave the ruling to me." He motioned for his horse and leapt into the saddle. In a flurry of hooves, the horses wheeled around and the coronation entourage galloped down the hill, leaving the bishop sputtering in a cloud of dust.

The bishop shook his cassock and led his monks and the young boy back along the Ridgeway towards the monastery.

Only Ethrelda was left. Sadly she searched the trampled ground for the pieces of the talisman. One glinted from the grass. She pounced and held it to her heart while looking for its mate. At first she could find nothing. Then a tiny gleam made her scrape away some soil in a hoofprint. There was the second half, trodden deep into the dirt.

Ethrelda rubbed the gold pieces clean on her shift and butted the edges together. She sighed. "A smith could forge you, but I have no skills. The bishop smote you, and no man will go against him. I must hide you."

Concealing the pieces in her palm, Ethrelda darted beyond the ditch and ran across the hillside towards the White Horse carving.

⧈ ⧈ ⧈

Quick! Follow her! Chantel leaned forward over the horse's neck.

Of course, said the White Horse. *But like you, Ethrelda is a Magic Child. Your time and hers must not mix. Stay silent so she does not sense your presence.*

I will, Chantel promised.

The White Horse cantered slowly alongside Ethrelda, then stood at the head of his carving.

⧈ ⧈ ⧈

Ethrelda looked around. The camps were empty. The few people perched on top of the embankment were watching the revelries inside the earthworks. She stepped across the carved lines of the horse and knelt by the giant white eye.

"I feel your presence, Horse King," Ethrelda whispered. "You feel so near."

Chantel leaned forward and stroked the horse's neck.

He blew gently through his nostrils. Chantel's mouth opened in a silent gasp as Ethrelda's hair stirred with his breath.

"Take back your talisman, Horse King. Though your magic is fading, may it never die," Ethrelda whispered as she scrabbled a small hole deep into the chalk.

Wait.

Ethrelda cocked her head on one side as though listening to an invisible voice.

You are wise beyond your years, Ethrelda. I thank you for recovering the talisman, but bury only one piece here. The red mare and I must be forever linked. To strengthen our link you must bury the other half of the talisman with her. Hide it in the chalk taken to fill the red mare's eye at the time of our next scouring.

"I will," whispered Ethrelda. She dropped one gold piece in the hole, replaced the scrapings and stamped them down hard with her foot. The second piece she knotted into the hem of her shift for safety.

"Goodbye, Horse King. I will do as you ask. May you and the red mare always run together." Ethrelda looked around again; no one had observed her. She ran back into the great earthworks, where she mingled with the crowd.

❖ ❖ ❖

The images wavered and the sunshine faded away. Chantel and the White Horse stood alone on the midnight hilltop.

Was the other half of the talisman buried in the eye of the red mare? asked Chantel.

Equus blew a gusty sigh through his nostrils. *It was. Ethrelda was true to her word. If you find the red mare, you will find the other half of my talisman."*

So there really is a Red Horse Vale?

Yes, the vale is there still, though it has changed. The beautiful red mare and her foal vanished, and with her much of the horse magic. Find her, so she and I can ride the wind together and the old magic awaken further. If my talisman is found and made whole, the old magic will be even stronger.

Chantel patted the horse's neck. *I'll try to help you.*

The hooves of the White Horse struck the downs and horse and child took to the air, leaping through sunsets and sunrises, jumping the stars and swooping through swirling galaxies. They galloped together until the heavens rang with Chantel's laughter. Eventually, breathless and exhausted, she shouted, "ENOUGH!"

The White Horse paused on a silvery mountaintop.

Where are we? Chantel asked.

The Place Beyond Morning. What do you see?

Chantel looked around and smiled. *A land of silver. It's pretty.*

Equus sighed. *Are you tired, child?*

Chantel nodded. *Yes. It's hard to hold on.*

Then lie along my neck. We will return.

Chantel lay forward along the smooth white neck, clasping her arms around it. Sleepily she rubbed her cheek against the warm skin and smiled, as she smelled the horse's musky scent. His muscles bunched beneath her and the air streamed past, lifting strands of mane to tickle her face. A smile still on her face, Chantel felt her eyelids droop. She slept.

"I took the child to the Place Beyond Morning," said Equus.

"Did she understand?" Ava asked.

Equus shook his head "How could she? All she saw was silvery beauty. She didn't recognize the emptiness." He sighed. "She is so young. Everything in her world is new to her. How can she understand what is happening in the universe? Even we were vanquished because we didn't understand in time."

Myrddin grunted in protest. "Not vanquished. We retreated! Our land is still there. We will be back. We must go back. The balance must be kept. Light and dark ...There must always be light and dark."

"But the dark is such a fearful dark," Ava cried. "The Dark Being has grown so powerful that now the light is extinguished where she passes."

"Take heart, Ava. Even the Dark Being could not permanently darken the Place Beyond Morning. Though empty, it shines still," said Equus.

Ava ruffled her feathers uneasily. "For how long? Last night I saw a small star go out. The Dark Being has become stronger. We must find a way to become stronger too."

"We will. My heart tells me the other children will soon hear me and help."

"Take care with the humans, Equus," Myrddin cautioned. "As they waken our old magic, the Dark Magic stirs. Dark and light, light and dark. There cannot be one without the other. The human children may not recognize which is which. Take great care."

CHAPTER FIVE

FOUR FOR A BOY

While Chantel slept in her hospital bed, Adam tossed and turned in the lower bunk. Owen slept peacefully on the top, but Adam couldn't sleep. He was wrestling with his conscience.

He had known looking after Chantel in England would be a pain, but now things were really awful.

It's not her fault, suggested the voice of his conscience, but Adam knew it was. If Chantel hadn't whined to be included, if his mother hadn't been on her side, then Chantel wouldn't have come to England and fallen! Now instead of Owen and him having fun together, they were making stupid trips to the hospital.

"It's not fair," Adam said out loud as he thumped his pillow angrily into another shape. "She spoils everything." He slammed his head on the pillow. He was sick of his mom and dad dumping Chantel on him. They were always fighting and wanting her out of the way. Then when things went wrong they blamed him. It wasn't fair. He wasn't Chantel's parent. He was a ten-year-old kid.

A surge of anger washed over him. He was angry with his parents and their secret discussions about a "trial separation." As if he didn't know! He was angry with Chantel and angry with himself for being angry with her. He was scared too, really scared. Divorce was scary, and what if it was his fault?

Adam took a deep breath and closed his eyes. He blocked out the bad thoughts and conjured the horse pasture on a bright sunny afternoon. He and Owen were exercising the racehorses. He rode so well that Uncle Ron asked him to be a jockey in the next race. The race took place, and in a flurry of pounding hooves he won!

Adam's eyes sprang open as the memory of the real gallop across the hillside intruded. His frustration level rose again. Huh! he thought. Chantel falls and we all think she's dead. Then she goes on about a magic horse and Holly and Owen believe her. It's nuts.

What if it's true? whispered a voice.

Adam tossed and turned again. *How can it be true?* he retorted. *Auntie Lynne said Chantel might hallucinate. That's what she's doing!*

What about the broken token and her knowing about Wayland's Smithy? answered the irritating little voice.

I don't know, admitted Adam wearily. His hand crept under his pillow and found the half-talisman he'd placed there. He wasn't sure why he'd put it under his pillow. It just seemed the right thing to do. He clasped it angrily in his palm. *I'm fed up with being messed around. I wish I could do something about it.*

Suddenly he became aware of something stirring in the darkness, not a real thing, more of a dark presence inside his head.

You can. I'll help you, said the voice calmly.

Adam broke out in a sweat. This voice wasn't his conscience. It was something else!

All magic is quite simple, really, continued the voice. *Anger is good. It makes you feel with passion. Feel your anger as you clasp the talisman.*

Suddenly, Adam found himself outside, surrounded by the soft darkness of night. He was not scared, just amazed. The velvet sky arched above him. A million stars sparkled. As his eyes adjusted, Adam recognized his surroundings. He was standing on the flat top of a small conical hill. The flank of White Horse Hill towered above him, and the valley called the Manger lay below.

"Holy mackerel! I'm on Dragon Hill. How on earth? Who brought me here? Who *are* you?" Adam shouted, spinning around.

With a soft chuckle, the voice in his head spoke again.

I am the dragon. Some call me Worm. I am an ancient magic. I was old when the White Horse carving was young. But all that's remembered of me are fragments of stories. It's not the White Horse who needs help, boy. Its image is there for all to see. I, Worm, need your help. The dragon's voice grew shrill. *My need is greatest. I am trapped.* He paused, then spoke again, softly and sweetly. *I am almost lost to human memory. Please help me.*

Adam shifted uneasily. The White Horse had said something similar to Chantel.

Worm read his mind. *We can show ourselves because there is a new Magic Child. Through her the old magic is stirring. She gave you the broken talisman.* The dragon laughed softly. *She did not tell you that whoever holds it holds power. Now you hold the talisman. It is strong and powerful, and your anger makes you strong and powerful. You attracted my magic as it began to stir. I grew strong enough to bring you here.*

Adam was aware of the talisman in his hand. It felt warm. He opened his palm. The gold piece gave off a soft beam of light. Adam's anger stirred deep within him. How dare Chantel hide power from him?

That's good, whispered Worm. *Let your anger fuel my dragon magic. Watch the light.*

The beam from the token became stronger. A flickering image appeared in its light. Adam cupped his hands and bent closer. A beautiful, blood-red dragon flew in the beam. A laughing boy was perched on his back between his shimmering wings. The boy turned his head. He was Adam.

Adam gasped.

Yes. This could be you, whispered Worm's sly voice. *The Magic Child has the horse. Wouldn't you like the dragon?*

Yes ... Yes ... I'd love to fly like that. But where are you? How come I can only see you in this beam of light?

My magic is not yet strong enough. But old magic can be strengthened in many ways. One is to become a believer. We need many believers. Another way is to find and join the broken talisman. If you find the other half, boy, you will have power undreamed of. Until you do, keep this half safe. Sleep with it in your hand again, and I will bring you once more to Dragon Hill. What's your name, boy?

Adam.

Adam ... Adam. The dragon rolled the name around his tongue. *A fitting name. It means first born. Adam, you shall be the first holder of the dragon magic. Names are powerful, Adam. You must use mine. Call me Worm and our bond will deepen.*

I could teach you words of power, Adam. Ancient and secret words that summon me. Unless they are spoken by the holder of the talisman, I will remain imprisoned beneath your feet. Once I am free we will share magic. Free me, Adam, and you too can have power. The power to do anything. The power to change things however you wish.

Adam staggered, almost overcome by the possibilities that flashed before him. He could stop his parents from fighting. He could stop Chantel from bugging him. He chuckled. He could turn her into a beetle! He could live on his own with Owen and they could do whatever they liked. He could have loads of money. Yes. He would free the dragon and together they would fix the whole world.

Adam gazed in wonder at the bald earth beneath his feet. *Dragon Hill ... you're inside Dragon Hill! Amazing! Tell me what to do and ... and ... I'll let you out. We'll fly around the world together and fix things.*

The dragon chuckled again. *You are the eager one!* His voice grew serious. *But there is a price, Adam. To gain the power you must bring me the whole talisman.*

But ...

No time to argue, said Worm firmly. *Bring me both halves of the talisman and I will show you how to use them. Say nothing to the others. Dragon magic is old and fragile until I can reappear and strengthen it. See, my image is failing.*

The flickering dragon in the beam of light was fading.

Quick, clasp the talisman — I must return you. Come again another night.

Adam folded his hand and cut off the glow. Darkness surrounded him, and he was filled with a sense of loss.

Close your eyes and think of where you came from. The dragon's voice was a faint whisper. Adam closed his eyes tightly and imagined lying in his bunk bed in the farmhouse.

❈ ❈ ❈

A hand grasped his shoulder and shook hard. "Come on, Adam. Wakey, wakey! We're going to Wayland's Smithy today, remember?"

Groggily, Adam opened his eyes to find Owen leaning over him.

"You were dead to the world," Owen laughed. "I've been trying to wake you for ages. Come on, breakfast's ready."

During breakfast Adam hardly spoke. His mind was full of his dream. He refused eggs, chewed through a bowl of cereal and reached for some toast.

The phone rang.

"It's your mother." Holly handed the mobile receiver to Adam.

Adam's face lit up. He grabbed the phone. "Hi, Mom!"

"Are you okay?" His mother's voice sounded distant, with a tinny echo at the end of each sentence.

"I'm fine. And Chantel's getting better. I went to see her yesterday and we'll go again today."

"What on earth were you all doing?" his mother said. "Chantel shouldn't have been riding. She's only seven."

"What do you mean?" Adam's smile faded. "You let her ride. We all went trail riding last summer."

"Yes, but I was there. So was your dad. You shouldn't have been out on horses on your own. I told you to look after your sister."

"Auntie Lynne and Uncle Ron let us. Holly and Owen ride everywhere."

"They're older. I expected you to use some common sense."

"Mom, it wasn't my fault. We were all doing fine. The lightning startled the horse. That's why Chantel fell." Adam's voice rose. "No one can help lightning." He hunched over the receiver and turned his back on his cousins.

Holly and Owen stared at each other across the table.

"Adam said they blame him," Owen mouthed.

Holly nodded. She busied herself with toast. Owen did the same. The distant voice on the phone droned on and on.

Adam suddenly pushed the off button, and dropped the phone on the table.

"You okay?" asked Owen.

Adam looked at him, his face white. He shook his head and walked upstairs.

Holly and Owen watched until he disappeared.

"That sounded awful," whispered Holly.

Owen agreed. "Poor Adam. He had a bad night too. He

tossed and turned for ages. He was real hard to wake up this morning."

Holly looked around. Her dad had left for the barns and she could hear her mother in another room. She dropped her voice further. "I wonder if Adam overheard Mum and Dad talking. I did."

"You did? You eavesdropped? What did they say?"

"It was an accident," said Holly. She beckoned Owen closer. "I thought everyone was asleep. I came down to the fridge for some milk, and they were talking in the living room with the door open. If I tell you what they said, promise not to tell?"

"Cross my heart or hope to die," said Owen, swiftly crossing his chest with his finger.

Holly bent close to Owen's ear. "Aunt Celia and Uncle Brent might be getting a divorce," she hissed. "That's why Adam and Chantel are visiting England on their own."

"When they go back to Canada, their mum and dad will be divorced?" Owen's eyes were wide with shock.

"Shhhhhh." Holly shook her head. "Not quite. Chantel and Adam are here so Aunt Celia and Uncle Brent can have time together to try and work things out."

Owen let out his breath in a whoosh of air. "Phew. Poor Chantel and Adam."

"Don't say anything. But maybe that's why Adam and his family are angry all the time."

Owen turned and looked at the stairs. "I should go and see if he's all right."

"You promised not to say anything!" Holly grabbed Owen's arm. "You promised."

"Keep your hair on. I'm not stupid," said Owen, shaking her hand off.

"Well, don't go yet," Holly insisted. "Leave it a bit. So it doesn't look like you're being nosy."

Owen nodded slowly. "All right. A divorce, though. Wow! Are they supposed to choose between their mum and dad? That's not fair." He wandered out of the kitchen, looking dazed.

⚔ ⚔ ⚔

Adam threw himself on his bunk. His mom was mad at him again. He'd figured she would be. Chantel was her favorite. Dad's too. Everything blurred as his eyes watered. A lump formed in his throat. He thumped the pillow with his fist. "It wasn't my fault, it wasn't my fault, it wasn't my fault!" he said.

After a while he stood up and wandered over to the window. He stared into the distance with his hand in his pocket, absently turning the talisman over and over.

He pulled out the piece of gold. "Do I ever wish my dream was real, that you truly had magical powers," he whispered to himself. "Oh boy, would I change my life!"

The talisman lay still and silent in his palm.

Adam looked up again at the rolling swell of the downs beyond the farm. He considered the possibility of magic. "My little sister says she's talked to the White Horse, and I dreamed about a dragon imprisoned in Dragon Hill. We must both be going nuts."

He looked down at the broken talisman again and shrugged. "All right, I'll take you to this Wayland's Smithy place," he said. He leaned his head against the cool glass on the windowpane. "Let's hope nothing happens. Then I'll know for sure that Chantel's been hallucinating, and I just had a crazy dream. Stress, that must be what's causing it ... stress."

The lump in his throat grew larger and a dry sob escaped. He swallowed and muttered fiercely, "But if the talisman is real, then the dragon magic is real. If I make the talisman whole and free the dragon, I can use the power."

Adam clenched his fist around the talisman and thrust his arm in the air. "I'll fix my parents," he roared. "I'll fix everyone and everything. I'll fix the whole darned world so no one is ever unhappy again!" Then his body sagged, the lump in his throat grew too big, and for the first time in years Adam cried.

Owen paused outside the bedroom door, his hand on the knob. He heard the muffled sob, sat down on the stairs and waited until all was quiet.

🔲 🔲 🔲

The sun shone brilliantly. Adam's spirits rose as he followed Owen and Holly to the stables. He didn't care what his mother said. He was going riding!

The ponies whickered a greeting. Adam slapped Mischief's rump. She moved over so he could curry-comb her coat; then she turned and nuzzled his pockets for the carrot she knew would be there.

After grooming and saddling up, Adam and his two cousins rode sedately through Uffington. Adam gazed around with interest. Seated on Mischief he could see over hedges and into the gardens of the thatched cottages. The cottages were old, with wavy roofs and black timbers standing out starkly against the whitewashed walls. It was like riding through a storybook.

Holly and Owen waved to several people, who smiled and waved back. Then the road curved around the grounds of the Big House. They clopped past the church and the Blowing Stone Inn.

"The Blowing Stone?" questioned Adam as they passed under the painted inn sign. "Chantel mentioned a Blowing Stone in her dream." He pointed upward. The painting showed what looked like a man bending over a gigantic stone. "Why is that dude kissing a rock?"

Holly and Owen reined in their ponies and turned to look up at the sign.

Owen grinned. "It's supposed to be King Alfred blowing into the stone. He doesn't look much like a king, though, does he?"

Adam shook his head.

Holly squinted up. "He has a gold band on his head. My history teacher says that was a crown in Alfred's time."

"So ... what's this Alfred dude doing?"

"He's making the stone sound like a trumpet." Holly looked at Adam. "You do know who Alfred was, don't you?"

Adam shook his head.

"He was the greatest of the Saxon kings," said Owen. "The one who burnt the cakes."

Adam still looked blank.

"Anyway, he was really important in English history," continued Owen. "And village stories say he was crowned around here ... in Uffington ... or maybe up there on White Horse Hill."

"Mind you, the people of Wantage say he was crowned there," interrupted Holly. "No one really knows, but everyone agrees it was somewhere around here. The Blowing Stone was on top of White Horse Hill inside Uffington Castle. For thousands of years it was sounded as a warning when there were raids on the fort or to celebrate things like Alfred's coronation. The sound carried for miles and miles and warned everyone. The inn sign shows Alfred blowing into the stone." She paused and looked up at the sign. "I don't know if Alfred really blew it, though."

Adam smirked. "So you really believe there once was a big rock that had a hole in it. And it made a noise like a trumpet that everyone could hear for miles and miles. Yeah, right!"

"Several holes, actually, but most of them are bunged up with dirt," laughed Holly.

"You mean ... ?" Adam stared at her.

Holly nodded. "Yup. The Blowing Stone is real. It was dragged down from the hill to the village years ago."

"People said it made too much noise up there when the wind blew," laughed Owen. "It's in a cottage garden at the crossroads. Want to see it?"

"You're having me on."

Holly and Owen grinned at each other and urged their ponies forward. Adam followed. They hacked through the village, along the lane and up to the crossroads. Holly dismounted and led Harlequin onto the grass verge, where she tied the reins to the bars of a gate.

Adam and Owen followed suit.

"This way, Adam," Owen called as he and Holly climbed a stile into a small cottage garden.

"This is someone's yard. Should we be in here?" Adam hesitated halfway over the stile.

Owen pointed out a small notice tacked onto a post. "It's a historic site. We're allowed to visit this part of the garden."

Holly patted a chest-high rock sitting in the middle of an unkempt lawn. "This is the Blowing Stone. See if you can make it work."

"You mean blow into it?"

Holly and Owen nodded.

Adam walked around the stone. It was riddled with large holes and hollows, some full of dirt. A fern grew out of one hole and drooped artistically down the side.

The stone was an irregular shape, but the top surface was roughly flat. Adam ran his hand over it. Then he spotted what he was looking for: in one corner was a small hole the size of a quarter. It was unlike the other sharp-edged holes and hollows. The rock around the edges of this hole was worn smooth and shiny. He stuck his finger in it. "Is this where you are supposed to put your mouth? It'll never work."

Holly and Owen grinned.

Adam bent forward, gingerly placed his lips around the hole and blew hard several times. Nothing happened. Red cheeked with effort, he straightened up to catch his breath.

"You have to make a seal all around the edge of the hole," encouraged Holly. "Then try with your lips pursed. Like blowing a trumpet. But you need more air."

"Just blow a gigantic raspberry," advised Owen.

Adam laughed, took in an enormous lungful of air, pursed his lips, bent down and blew as hard as he could.

A sputtering moan echoed through the garden.

Four startled magpies burst out of a nearby hawthorn tree, squawking angrily, and landed on the cottage roof.

"Four for a boy," chanted Holly, clapping. "Adam, this just might be your lucky day!"

Flushed with success, Adam blew again. The note was louder and longer but still not as impressive as he expected. "It makes a weird noise."

"Yup. Sounds like a sick cow." Owen grinned. "Go on ... try once more. Pretend you're King Alfred. But I bet you can't make a sound that can be heard all around the vale."

Adam stretched up and breathed heartily several times. He walked around the stone again. "I think some of these holes have been stopped up on purpose," he said. "That's what makes it so hard to blow." He picked up a small stick and cleared several of the cavities around the side. Finally he sucked in an enormous breath and bent over the Blowing Stone once again.

BRoooooooooooooooooooooooooooooom!

The magpies took off in fright, and an astounded Holly clapped her hands over her ears. With a shout of laughter Owen headed for the stile as the note echoed and re-echoed around the garden, through the village and up over the downs.

"Holy mackerel," said Adam, amazed. "That's loud enough to raise the dead. No wonder some holes were blocked."

"Amazing! I've never known anyone make that loud a sound. Come on, let's get out of here in case we've made folks mad," said Owen as he swung over the stile.

"Or scared the ponies," chuckled Holly.

Laughing, Adam hurried after them.

CHAPTER SIX

WAYLAND'S SECRET

The children rode uphill towards the Ridgeway and trotted through a gap in the bank. After passing the White Horse and Uffington Castle, they found themselves on a more sheltered track. It followed the flank of the downs and was edged by low banks and occasional clumps of trees. Gradually it dropped closer to the valley, and soon the ponies were winding their way through a small wood.

Holly pointed, and Adam glimpsed a squirrel scampering along a tree bough. Next Owen waved them all to a stop, and children and ponies watched as a fox, belly low to the ground, sped across the trail, through the trees and slipped out of sight along the edge of the field beyond.

"I've never seen a real fox before," Adam whispered.

"Well, keep your eyes peeled. There are badgers here

too," Holly whispered back.

Owen gave a muffled snort. "You don't see them in daylight. Only in the evenings."

"You never know," said Holly defensively. "We could be lucky. We don't often see foxes either."

They rode on without incident for about a mile. The track rose and fell. Only once did they need to pull the ponies to the side to allow a string of eight exercising race-horses to trot past. The ponies whickered a greeting, but the thoroughbreds merely twitched their ears in reply.

"How far is Wayland's Smithy?" asked Adam as they carried on.

"You can almost see it in the middle of the clump of trees ahead." Holly pointed.

Adam's stomach cramped with unease. He was almost at Wayland's Smithy, an old burial place said to be built by a blacksmith god. In a few minutes he'd find out if he and Chantel were crazy, or, worse still, if his dragon experience was real.

Mischief tossed her head nervously as Adam jagged the bit in her mouth. "Sorry, Mischief," he muttered, and slackened the reins. But his knuckles and face were white. It took courage to give her the signal to turn off the Ridgeway and follow the others through a gate into a small fenced wood.

Mischief stepped delicately into the area known as Wayland's Smithy. The trees thickened, then suddenly widened out. Adam found himself in a hidden clearing. He slid from Mischief's back and gazed around.

Holly slipped off her pony, looped Harlequin's reins up over his neck and tied them in a loose knot so he wouldn't trip on them. She gave him a friendly slap on the rear. "We can let the ponies roam. It's fenced," she called as she closed the gate. The two boys followed her example and the three ponies ambled into the shade of the trees.

The soft leafy ground and springy turf muffled the children's footsteps and the pony's hooves. A circle of majestic beech trees ringed a clearing, standing guard over the barrow and holding back the woodland. The children stepped between the beeches into the magic circle. No birds sang. No breeze stirred or leaves rustled. They had entered a bubble of silence.

Adam stared.

The barrow, a long, low, turf-covered mound, almost filled the beech-edged circle. The narrow end of the mound faced them, framed by two enormous stones. Beneath the lintel gaped a small dark hole.

Adam gulped. He didn't like small dark tunnels. No way was he going in there. He shuffled his feet. His skin prickled with fear.

"Have you got Chantel's talisman?" asked Owen.

Adam's hand slipped inside the pocket of his jeans. He nodded but did not bring it out.

Owen held out his hand impatiently. "Let's have it."

Adam drew the piece of gold from his pocket, but held on tight. "What are we supposed to do?" he asked quietly.

Owen shrugged. "Guess we keep trying things till something happens."

"Like what?" Adam's voice squeaked with tension.

Holly crossed the turf and stood before the lintel stones.

"The stories say to leave a coin on the entrance stones if you want your horse shod," she said.

"We don't," Adam said flatly. "And it isn't a coin."

"Try it anyway." Holly pointed to a rock between the stones. "Put the talisman there."

Adam edged towards the dark entrance. His fingers didn't want to let go, but he dropped the talisman. It landed with a tinkle. Wave upon wave of mystery flowed from the dark tunnel, wrapping tendrils around his body and tugging him towards the entrance. Adam retreated fast.

Holly climbed casually on top of the burial mound. Owen also seemed unaffected by the atmosphere.

The talisman lay there. Nothing happened.

Owen fidgeted for a few moments, then walked over and picked it up. "Maybe someone has to take it inside."

A surge of relief swept over Adam. Yes ... it didn't have to be him. Let Owen go in the dark hole.

Owen held the talisman between his finger and thumb, bent double and slipped inside the barrow.

"Any skeletons in there?" Adam asked Holly.

She shook her head. "No. The burial chambers were excavated years ago." She jumped down from the side of the mound and ran back towards the lintels. "They took the skeletons to a museum somewhere." She looked at Adam and laughed. "It's not scary, silly. The entrance just leads to three little hollows. You can always see daylight, even from the deepest one." She bent down and peeked inside. "Anything happening?" she called.

"Not a thing," Owen's disembodied answer wafted up. He crawled out of the entrance and handed the talisman to Holly. "Try something else."

Holly looked around. "Chantel walked widdershins

around the eye. Let's try that." She ran past Adam to the entrance of the beech-tree circle, paused and, holding the talisman before her, walked slowly around the edge of the clearing in an anti-clockwise direction.

She made seven circles. Nothing happened.

Holly offered the talisman to Adam. "Your turn."

Adam shrank back. He had known that it would come to this. He was going to have to crawl in that hole. It was still pulling at him.

"Come on, Adam." Holly pressed the talisman into his palm. "What's the matter?"

"He's scared," Owen said, grinning.

Adam looked at them. "Don't you feel it?" he asked.

Owen stopped laughing. "Feel what?"

"As though ... as though the hole ... is trying to pull you inside?"

Holly and Owen stared at the entrance to the barrow and back at Adam.

Owen slowly shook his head. "I don't feel anything. Does it feel like that to you?"

"Yes," whispered Adam.

"Then it's got to be you who takes the talisman inside. Go on. We'll be right here. Yell if you need help, but you've got to try."

He pushed Adam towards the barrow.

Adam crouched in the entrance. It was dark, and smelled of damp rock. He was going to have to move if he wanted to see inside. His body was blocking the daylight.

He crawled forward. Loose stones and rocks poked into his hands and knees. Air swirled around him. The rocks throbbed gently, as if to a giant heartbeat. Or was it his heart thumping? Adam couldn't tell. His imagination worked overtime. What if a bat flew into his hair? What if he knelt on a snake? What if spiders fell down his neck? What if the magic sucked him in and he was never seen again? Heart pounding, he eased himself into a hollow on one side of the passage and let a shaft of sunlight through.

After his flights of imagination, Adam was relieved to see a short, well-trampled rocky passage opening into three alcoves made of gigantic slabs of rock. Interesting, but not scary.

"Anything happening?" yelled Holly from outside.

"No," Adam called back.

"Have you held up the talisman?"

"Not yet," he admitted.

"Come on, Adam. What are you waiting for?" Owen was getting impatient.

"All right. Here goes." Adam unclasped his hand and exposed the half-talisman.

For a moment it just lay there. Then it began to feel warm, and, just as it had in his dream, it started to glow.

"Are you okay, Adam?" called Holly.

Adam barely heard her. Magic filled the air. The rock slabs around him pulsed and throbbed with life. He reached out and touched the rock opposite.

It moved. The beam of light from the broken talisman lit the opening of a new passage.

Adam looked down the dark passage with horror. Dull red flames glimmered in the distance. Fear washed over him, fear of things lurking in small dark places. He turned towards the entrance to ask Owen and Holly for help but was stopped. Frantically he pushed with his hands and his shoulder. An invisible barrier blocked him from the entrance. He was trapped.

"THE BLOWER OF STONE MUST ENTER ALONE!" boomed a voice.

Adam shrank back.

"THE BLOWER OF STONE MUST ENTER ALONE!" boomed the voice again.

Adam took a deep breath. "I am alone," he said. His voice shook. "I'm Adam. I blew into the stone. Wh ... who are you?"

"I MAKE IRON BEND AND WATER FLY."

"You do?" said Adam, baffled.

"PROCLAIM MY NAME," continued the voice.

Adam groaned "Oh no, not a riddle. I'm no good at riddles. I need Holly and Owen." Once more he turned back, but the invisible wall held. He sank back, cracking his head on a rock. "Ouch!" he cried, rubbing the spot. "Okay, okay ... I'll try on my own." He pondered the riddle. Come on brain, think. Lots of people bend iron. But flying water? "Do you mean water going over a waterfall, or pouring water?" he called.

No answer.

Adam concentrated.

Who makes iron bend? he mused. People in factories, bridge builders, welders, blacksmiths, ironworkers ... yes, that was it! Blacksmiths, of course. The blacksmith makes iron bend when he's making horseshoes. And red-hot horseshoes are dunked into cold water ... which evaporates into steam ... so ... flying water! "Are you the blacksmith?" he called.

Still no reply.

But that had to be it. Adam thumped the rock in frustration. It was the only thing that made sense. He muttered the words to himself. "'I make iron bend, and water fly. Proclaim my name.' Oh ... I've got to name you ... and ... and ... this is Wayland's Smithy." Adam raised his voice. "Are you called Wayland?"

"ENTER, BLOWER OF STONE."

Adam moved forward. Nothing stopped him. "Let's get this over with," he muttered, and screwed up his courage. Holding the half-talisman up to light his way, he bent double and edged into the low entrance. With each step the red light grew stronger and the passage grew warmer. Soon he was dripping sweat. His heart beat so loudly, it was almost deafening. But was it his heart? Adam paused to listen. The tunnel glowed and pulsed with fiery red light. The noise was not his heartbeat; it was the rhythmic blowing of a gigantic bellows in a blacksmith's forge. The sound overwhelmed him. He could go no farther.

"WHO SENT YOU?" boomed the voice.

Adam thought for a moment. He mustn't mention the dragon. "Er ... The White Horse. We ... we ... were told to ... br ... bring the broken talisman here," Adam shouted.

"WHAT DO YOU SEEK?"

Adam shrugged. "The red mare, I guess. To find her for the White Horse and ..."

"AND?"

"Can you fix the talisman?" finished Adam, his voice shaking with effort and fear.

An image appeared on the fiery walls. Two halves of the talisman moved towards each other. They butted together.

FLASH! A light like a million fires blazed. CLANG! A giant hammer struck an anvil. The talisman on the wall shone whole. The design was clear, not one horse, but two galloping horses.

Adam stared.

Wayland spoke again:

"THOSE YOU SEEK ARE RUNNING STILL,
THOUGH HIDDEN NOW, BENEATH THE HILL.
WHAT LIES BELOW IS SEEN ON HIGH.
SEEK THEM WHERE THE MAGPIES FLY.

SEEK THEM AS SMALL SHADOWS, CAST
BY THE SUN WHEN NOON HATH PASSED.
RED LIKE WHITE IN SLUMBER LIE,
THE TALISMAN WITHIN THE EYE."

Adam struggled to take it all in.

The voice continued: "TAKE HEED YOU FIND NOT THAT YOU MUST NOT SEEK! SEEK INSTEAD HE WHO BEARS MY NAME."

Gradually the fiery glow on the walls, the talisman image, and the echo from the forge faded. The feeling of magic drifted away.

Adam found himself sitting in the rock alcove, clutching

the half-talisman. Holly and Owen peered in at him from beyond the lintel.

"So?" said Owen.

"So what?" said Adam.

"So, did you hold the talisman up?"

Adam gazed back at them. "Didn't you hear anything?" he asked.

"No," they chorused.

Adam stuck out one hand. "I've gotta get out of here. Please help me." His hand trembled.

Two arms grabbed Adam and he half crawled and was half dragged out of the hole. He sprawled on the turf, blinking up at Holly and Owen.

"How long was I in there?" he asked.

"Only a couple of minutes. What's the matter? Are you claustrophobic or something?" Holly asked.

"Weird ... really weird," Adam stammered. "Wasn't I in there for ages?"

Holly and Owen shook their heads.

Adam closed his eyes. "I must be going mad. Wayland spoke to me!"

CHAPTER SEVEN

ALL MIXED UP

Adam told about Wayland's voice and the new passage.

Owen and Holly gazed at the half-talisman.

"I never really believed ..." Holly whispered. She traced the partial design etched in the gold. "So this is part of two horses. Do you think it's the White Horse and his mate?"

The gate squeaked.

"Hello, hello, hello. Find something interesting?"

The three children jumped. Holly dropped the talisman back into Adam's palm. He stuffed it in his pocket as an elderly man with a walking stick strode into the clearing.

"Oh, hello, Mr. Smythe." Holly's smile was bright, but a red flush stained her cheeks.

"Er, hello, sir. W ... w ... what are you doing here?" stammered Owen.

"Taking my daily constitutional. I often march this way." Mr. Smythe twirled his stick. "I think of it as coming to see my ancestor!"

"You do?" said Holly. She looked across at Owen. He shrugged.

Mr. Smythe laughed and banged his stick on the lintel stone. "Wayland's Smithy ... and Smythe ... See?"

"Not really," admitted Holly.

"Smythe ... that's a corruption of smith. Having the name Smythe means my ancestors once were blacksmiths, like Wayland."

"Honest? Everyone called Smythe once had a blacksmith in the family?" Owen was intrigued.

Mr. Smythe nodded. "Might have been several centuries ago ... but occupations were often what gave people a last name. John the smith became John Smith, and Pete the miller became Peter Miller."

"What about the name Baker?" asked Holly. "I've a friend called Sandra Baker. Does that mean someone in her family made bread?"

"Probably," agreed Mr. Smythe. "Then there is the name Johnston — that was originally John's son. And Thomson was ..."

"Tom's son," finished Owen with delight. "Is this what you researched when you were a historian?"

Mr. Smythe laughed. "No. I analyzed aerial photos. I discovered archeological remains on the ground from clues that could only be seen from the air. But now I'm retired, I indulge myself with any research I fancy. Names have always fascinated me."

Mr. Smythe turned to Adam, who had been standing in

a daze. He stuck out his hand. "I live in the Big House in the village. You must be Adam; I heard you were coming. How's that little sister of yours?"

"She's going to be okay," Adam gasped as his hand was pumped up and down. He was not used to the idea that everyone in the country knew what was going on at the neighbors'. "We're going to visit her again this afternoon."

"Good, good." Mr. Smythe sat down on a protruding stone at the edge of the mound. He waggled his stick at Holly and Owen. "Anything I can do, you let me know, pronto! Can't have visitors to our fair country running into problems."

"We'll do that, sir." As Owen smiled his thanks he looked across at Holly and raised his eyebrows in a silent question. She gave a tiny nod. "Actually there is something, sir," Owen continued. "But it's a secret ... you have to promise not to tell if we show you."

Mr. Smythe stood up and saluted smartly. "Captain's honor."

Adam's heart sank to his boots. Surely Owen wasn't going to tell a grown-up about the talisman. A spark of anger flared. The Smythe man would take it, say it was important or something. Adults always took away interesting things; they could never be trusted. Adam heard Owen's voice, but it was as though he was speaking from far away.

"Well, sir ... Chantel ... that's Adam's sister ... the one in hospital." Owen paused, trying to get his thoughts straight.

Mr. Smythe nodded encouragingly.

"Well, she was given half an old coin ... She was told it was an old talisman ... and we are trying to find out about it. Want to see it?" Owen finished.

Adam's face flushed and his eyes sparked. How dare

Owen offer to show the talisman without asking?

Mr. Smythe twirled his cane and sat down again on his stone. "I'd be most interested."

That did it. Anger swept over Adam like a red tide. No way was he going to show the magic talisman to a strange adult. It was his now. He needed it for the dragon.

He spun on his heels and sprinted towards Mischief.

"Hey, Adam," shouted Owen in surprise. "What's up?" He set off in pursuit.

As Adam passed by, Holly stuck out her foot. Down he crashed. Owen, unable to stop, tripped over Adam's body and thumped down on top of him. Both boys gasped with pain. Owen rolled off Adam and sat up, rubbing his ribs. Adam turned on his side and pummeled Owen's back awkwardly with his fists.

"How could you?" Adam gasped between thumps. "Why? ... It isn't yours anyway ... We weren't to tell." He let fly with another volley of weak punches.

Owen rolled out of the way as Holly ran over and threw herself down on Adam's chest. She held his flailing arms. "Quit it, Adam Maxwell," she ordered. "Or I'll tell Mum you were fighting."

Adam subsided. He still gasped for breath, but the pain from being winded was wearing off. His anger burned bright and strong. He glared up at them. "You can't have it," he yelled. "It's not yours. It's mine! Mine and ..." He clamped his mouth shut.

"And whose?" asked Holly.

The color ebbed from Adam's face. In his fury he'd nearly blurted out about the dragon. He heaved his body to dislodge

Holly and rolled over again to lie face down, his head buried in his arms. If only Wayland would open up the ground and swallow him whole.

Holly and Owen clambered to their feet.

Mr. Smythe also stood. "Tell you what," he said as he brushed off the seat of his trousers. "Come and see me when you've sorted things out with your cousin. You know where I live." He strode out of the clearing, whistling.

Owen lifted his foot to kick Adam in the ribs.

"Don't!" shouted Holly.

"He started it," Owen muttered. "And he's lying there like a baby."

"Well don't you make it worse," Holly snapped, then turned and poked Adam with her own foot. "Come on, Adam, get up."

Owen gave a snort and pointed to Holly's outstretched boot.

Holly glanced down. "That's different," she said, grinning. "Oh, do get up, Adam," she said, chuckling and deliberately poking him with her foot again. "We didn't mean to upset you by telling Mr. Smythe. We just forgot you wouldn't know he's a friend. He often talks to us. We should have gone to see him earlier. He collects information about horse magic. Come on. Get up."

Adam rolled over and looked up at the two grinning faces.

"Come on, Adam. I'm sorry I tripped you."

Owen thrust out his hand to help Adam up. "We'll tell you all about Mr. Smythe if you tell us who else you think the talisman belongs to," he offered.

Adam grasped Owen's outstretched hand and rose stiffly

to his feet. But he refused to speak.

Holly stamped her foot.

"Adam Maxwell, you're a pain! I'm glad I tripped you. You've been a pain all day. You hardly spoke to us at breakfast, and now you've tried to run off with the talisman. It's not just yours, you know. And you've embarrassed us in front of a friend when all we are doing is trying to help."

Holly stomped over to her pony and unknotted the reins. "Okay, you're on your own. Come on, Owen. Let him stew." She led Harlequin through the gate.

Adam looked stonily at the ground.

Owen rolled his eyes and walked over to where Batman nibbled the grass. He mounted, and dug his heels into Batman's flanks. Batman tossed his head several times and followed Harlequin through the gate and out onto the Ridgeway.

Mischief whickered softly as the other ponies left. She ambled over to Adam and butted him in the back. He gave a half laugh, half sob and threw his arms around her neck. "Oh Mischief, what now? It's all real ... I think."

Adam tried to sort out his thoughts. He was in a mess. A gigantic mess. What was he going to do with the talisman? Chantel mustn't have it. She was only a little kid. It was powerful. Really powerful. So was the dragon. He and the dragon were going to use it to fix things.

Suddenly Wayland's words echoed in his head. "Take heed you find not that you must not seek!"

Why, oh why, did he think of the dragon when he heard those words? He knew all about Chinese dragons. They brought good luck. He'd been to the Dragon Festival in Edmonton's Chinatown. The Chinese even had a year of the dragon. So why did this English dragon make him feel guilty and uncomfortable?

He rubbed his cheek against Mischief's warm neck. He was so mixed up. He needed to concentrate, to remember everything that had happened in the tunnel. Then he could use the information to get power. He must not forget one word that Wayland had said. He whispered the verse under his breath:

> Those you seek are running still,
> Though hidden now, beneath the hill.
> What lies below is seen on high.
> Seek them where the magpies fly.

That must be a clue to finding the red mare. They must have to look from a great height or something.

> Seek them as small shadows, cast
> By the sun when noon hath passed.
> Red like white in slumber lie,
> The talisman within the eye.

So the talisman was in the eye. Hmm, that would make sense. That's where Chantel said she found the first half.

Then came the warning, "Take heed you find not that you must not seek!" And the command, "Seek one that bears my name."

"Guess I have to look for someone called Wayland," Adam sighed out loud.

He could think no more. He was on overload. He unknotted the reins and tried to mount Mischief. She moved around him, making him hop with one foot in the stirrup.

"Quit it, Mischief," he muttered. But, sensing that she had the upper hand, Mischief lived up to her name. Finally Adam gave up, walked her over to the gate and mounted from there.

He surveyed the beech grove one last time and gave an awkward salute. "Bye, Wayland," he whispered. He turned his back and urged Mischief to a trot. "Come on, Mischief, we'd better catch up with Holly and Owen."

❖ ❖ ❖

Holly and Owen rode slowly towards home.

"Do you think Adam made everything up?" asked Holly.

"Dunno. Why would he do that?" Owen answered.

"Because of all the attention Chantel is getting."

Owen thought for a moment. "You think he could have made up the story about Wayland because Chantel told us about Alin and the red mare?"

Holly nodded.

"Naw. Adam couldn't make up stuff like that."

They rode on for a while. Then Owen broke the silence.

"Why is all this happening to them anyway? They don't even live here. They're from Canada. We know more about the White Horse than they do."

Holly shrugged again. "I suppose it's the Magic Child stuff, because Chantel saw the shooting star and did the spell. But it doesn't seem fair. Nothing ever happens to us. We're just hanging around."

"Let's change it," said Owen eagerly. "Let's do something. Why don't we take the talisman to Mr. Smythe? He knows loads about the White Horse, and I bet he'll know if there is a red horse around here. Let's go and see him this evening. To heck with Adam."

"Adam won't agree."

"Who cares? He doesn't have the talisman anymore!" Owen jiggled something in his pocket.

"You have it?" Holly's eyes widened.

Owen smirked. "Yup. It fell out of his pocket when we were fighting. I figured it was our turn to look after it!"

⊠ ⊠ ⊠

"Hi." Adam paused in the stable doorway, holding Mischief's reins.

Holly stopped brushing down Harlequin and looked at him over her pony's back. She waited for him to say more.

Owen, Batman's saddle in his arms, kept walking towards the low beam on the far side of the stable. He slung the saddle over it and hung up the reins before turning. The two of them were obviously waiting for Adam to say something.

Adam considered his options. He needed their help to decode Wayland's words and get the rest of the talisman. He'd better apologize.

"Look ... I didn't mean to ignore you, or embarrass you. I just ..." Adam spread his hand out in a gesture of despair. "I don't even know what's happening to me. Weird things are going on and I can't stop them. Please help me."

"If you want our help, you're going to have to trust us, not get mad when we suggest something," said Holly.

Mischief thrust her nose between Adam's body and the

stable doorway and rudely pushed him against the wall. Everyone burst out laughing.

"Yes, Mischief, Adam's an idiot," said Owen, chuckling. "Settle your pony, Adam. We'll talk after."

"And we'll tell you why we're going to show the talisman to Mr. Smythe," added Holly.

Adam's hand went to his pocket. His face blenched.

"It's okay." Owen held up the talisman. "I've got it. It fell out on the grass while we were fighting." His bright eyes challenged Adam. "I'll look after it for a while. See if Holly and I can have some adventures like you Canadians!"

Adam stiffened. A wave of anger swept over him, so intense that he saw Owen through a red haze. How dare you, he thought, clenching his fists.

That's good. Feed your anger. We can use its power. Let the anger build. The dragon's voice spoke in his mind.

The anger burned deep inside him. He could feel it. Yes, he would use it! He would watch and wait, and get the talisman back when Owen wasn't looking. Then he'd meet the dragon again, and everyone had better watch out!

Adam forced himself to grin at Owen. He spoke carefully. "I guess that's fair. It was kind of given to all of us." He led Mischief into her stall. "Just you wait," he muttered under his breath. "I'll pay you back for this. Just you wait."

▨ ▨ ▨

"Something's wrong," said Myrddin. "I feel it."

Equus flicked his ears and Ava cocked her head on one side. They concentrated.

"The Dark Being approaches, but she is still a long way off," murmured Ava.

"No, the disturbance comes from much closer, from Gaia," insisted Myrddin.

The three gazed down at the misty blue planet.

Equus nodded. "Yes ... I feel it too. The Old Magic is waking. It has disturbed the Dark Magic."

Myrddin nodded sadly. "Light and dark, the never-ending struggle."

Equus flicked his ears again as he listened intently. "There is dissension among the children. The dragon has spoken."

"I feared this moment," Myrddin groaned. "Humans cannot withstand the dragon. He speaks with honeyed tongue but causes great anger and feeds on the results."

"Do not give up hope," soothed Ava. "Human children have hidden strengths. But be ready, Equus. Go as soon as you are summoned."

"I am always ready," said Equus. "I will call for your help if the dragon's Dark Magic grows too strong." He gave a great sigh. "We should never have surrendered our tools."

"Hush," soothed Ava. "What is done was done for a purpose. By giving up our magic freely, we weakened the Dark Being's power for eons."

"But Equus is right," said Myrddin. "Our situation is dire. A people who have long forgotten us guard our tools, yet we cannot intrude in their lives without their invitation. Only one small child believes in Equus. Without more believers we cannot retrieve our tools. This time the Dark Being may conquer all."

"Never," said Ava with conviction. "Give the children time."

CHAPTER EIGHT

FIVE FOR SILVER

Owen and Holly rushed down the hospital corridor and burst into Chantel's hospital room. Adam followed. Owen tossed the talisman into Chantel's hand and leapt on the end of the bed.

Hands flew out to protect her leg.

"I was being careful," he said defensively.

"So ... did something happen?" asked Chantel eagerly.

"It did to Adam," said Holly. "It's a really weird story."

Chantel looked across at her brother. She grinned with relief. "If weird things are happening to you too, then I'm not crazy."

Adam shrugged. He slouched down on the chair, embarrassed at being the center of attention.

"Well? What happened? Tell me!" Chantel demanded.

Slowly, Adam began to relate what had happened to him at Wayland's Smithy.

Chantel smiled at her brother. "You were brave, Adam. You hate dark tunnels."

Adam twitched with embarrassment and glared at Owen, daring him to comment.

Chantel's finger traced the horse design. "So Wayland showed you the completed talisman and there are two horses on it. Just like the ones I saw in my dream last night."

"Another dream?" said Owen.

Chantel nodded. "The White Horse took me into the past and I saw a carving of two horses on the side of a hill, in a place called the Vale of the Red Horse."

"I've never heard of the Vale of the Red Horse," said Holly. She turned to Owen. "Have you?"

Owen shook his head. "Could be an old name that got forgotten when the horses disappeared."

"But how could the horses disappear?" asked Adam. "The White Horse carving is still there. If the red horse was carved into the hillside, why isn't she still there?"

Holly and Owen shrugged.

"The red mare and her foal were carved in the hillside. Just like the White Horse," said Chantel positively. "I saw them, and watched King Alfred's coronation. And I heard the Horse King telling Ethrelda where to put the talisman after the bishop broke it." Chantel described her latest dream about Alfred.

"We've got so many bits of information from the dreams and Wayland," said Owen. "I think we should go over them before it gets too confusing."

"It's kind of like doing a jigsaw." Holly grinned. "I'm good at jigsaws."

"Okay." Owen took charge. "Fit everything together no matter how daft it sounds." He held up a finger. "One, Chantel promises to help the White Horse find his mate the red horse and her foal. Right?"

Chantel nodded. "And I find half the talisman."

"Yeah ... you promised to look for that too, I guess." Owen frowned. "It's getting complicated already."

"No, it's not. It's just two parts of the same thing," argued Holly. "So the next thing is when the White Horse gives Chantel dreams. Clues are in the dreams."

"Like Alin's hill carving. That's what we're looking for," Chantel said.

"And it's carved in red clay, so it's not on the chalk downs," Owen added.

"And we know what it looks like because Adam saw it at Wayland's Smithy and I saw it in my Alfred dream," Chantel said.

"What about all the magic things, like the Blowing Stone? That was in one of the dreams," interrupted Adam. "If I hadn't blown the stone I don't think Wayland would have spoken to me."

"You're right. We're going to have to notice everything," Owen agreed.

"Like the magpies," added Holly.

Everyone stared at her.

"Haven't you noticed the magpies?" Holly sounded surprised. "Every time something happens to one of us or Chantel dreams something, the magpies are there ... like in the fortune-telling rhyme." She grinned and chanted.

> One for sorrow, two for joy,
> Three for a girl, four for a boy,
> Five for silver, six for gold,
> Seven for a secret never been told.

"I think we're up to four magpies. We haven't seen five yet, have we?" Holly checked around with everyone. "Unless Chantel or Adam have seen them in their adventures?"

Brother and sister shook their heads.

"So that's something we have to watch for. The magpies always tell of something important," Holly finished.

Owen's face glowed. "This is getting really exciting. Now if we can solve Wayland's riddle, we're set."

"What was it Wayland said?" asked Chantel. She rubbed her forehead. "My brain is too woolly to remember."

Everyone looked at Adam. He started chanting and Holly and Owen softly joined in.

> Those you seek are running still,
> Though hidden now, beneath the hill.
> What lies below is seen on high.
> Seek them where the magpies fly.
>
> Seek them as small shadows, cast
> By the sun when noon hath passed.
> Red like white in slumber lie,
> The talisman within the eye.

There was a long pause.

"That seems to say we'll find the red horse ... if we fly

like magpies ... in the afternoon," said Holly slowly. "And that the talisman is in its eye, like it was at the White Horse."

"So ... how are we going to fly?" asked Owen.

The cousins looked at each other and shrugged.

"Come back to that later. What about 'hidden now beneath the hill?'" asked Owen.

"Do you think the red horse could be hidden under Dragon Hill?" wondered Holly.

Adam started guiltily, but no one noticed.

Chantel shook her head. "The hill I saw was a big one, in a different valley."

"Besides, Dragon Hill is white chalk, not red clay," Owen pointed out.

"You're right ... that doesn't fit. But if the carvings were buried somewhere else it would fit," said Holly excitedly. "The images would still be running if they were just covered up. And if they are covered up, that's why no one knows about them."

Adam looked doubtful. "If they are covered up, how can they cast shadows?"

Chantel shrugged again. "Dunno. What else did Wayland say, Adam?"

Reluctantly, he quoted, "Take heed you find not that you must not seek. Seek instead he who bears my name."

"Hmm. I wonder what we are not supposed to be seeking. We've not come across anything to avoid so far," said Holly.

They haven't met the dragon, thought Adam uneasily. He suppressed the thought.

"Never mind that. We'll figure it out," said Owen. "But we have to talk to Mr. Smythe." He grinned cockily.

"Why?" asked Chantel.

"Mr. Smythe interrupted us at Wayland's Smithy," said Owen. Chantel nodded.

"Well," continued Owen, "he was telling us about people's occupations. How they turned into last names. John the smith became John Smith, and Pete the miller became Peter Miller."

"That's neat," said Chantel.

Owen laughed. "It gets better. He told us that his name, Smythe, was just a fancy way of saying smith and that his ancestors were blacksmiths. So, that's who we've got to see. Wayland says 'Seek instead he who bears my name' and who should turn up but Mr. Smythe ... the blacksmith!" Owen turned to Adam "See ... I told you!" he crowed.

"It kind of makes sense," Adam admitted reluctantly. "But Mr. Smythe won't believe us. No adult will."

"We won't tell him everything," said Owen. "Just that Chantel was given the talisman and we've heard something about a red horse vale. He collects stories like that all the time."

"That's true," said Holly. "Mr. Smythe talks to strangers in pubs and visits the old people in the village. He won't think there is anything weird in our questions. We ask him about stuff all the time. He's a friend."

"Okay. Just ask him about the red horse," agreed Chantel. "But what about Wayland's warning?" Chantel shifted uneasily. "There must be something we are not supposed to look for." She glanced across at her brother with sudden intuition. "Is there something you're not telling, Adam?"

Adam flushed angrily. "No!" He glared around, daring someone to argue with him.

Chantel dropped her eyes.

Adam clenched his hands. His little sister sensed something. Too bad. He wasn't going to tell them. He was going to fly with the dragon and use its power. They might not be able to fly, but he and the dragon could. Then he could find the red horse on his own!

"You yelled that the talisman was yours, yours and ... then you stopped," Owen suddenly remembered. "You were planning to take it to someone else, weren't you?" He glared accusingly at Adam.

Adam glared back.

Chantel covered the talisman with her blanket.

"Oh nice, really nice," Adam said. "Now you've turned my little sister against me."

"Give over, you two." Holly's hand cut the air between them. "You were such friends yesterday. What changed?"

"He did," said both boys, pointing at each other.

Chantel stifled a giggle as the boys turned to glare at her. She took the broken talisman from under the blanket and offered it to Holly. "Why don't you show it to Mr. Smythe this evening? You're the only one who hasn't kept it for a while." She smiled. "The doctors say I can come home tomorrow morning. You can tell me what happens then."

"You're coming home!" Holly shrieked with delight. Owen double-slapped Chantel's hands.

Adam's smile hid his smoldering anger.

It was early evening and still light out as Holly led the way through the gates of the Big House and up the broad sweep of gravel drive.

"Mr. Smythe must be rich," Adam said as he took in the enormous lawn and the impressive terrace and columns along the front of the house.

"He doesn't act rich," said Owen. "The house has been in his family forever, but he kind of lives in the kitchen and doesn't use the other rooms, except for special occasions."

They ignored the steps up to the imposing front door, skirted a flowerbed and started down a narrow flag path that ran along the side of the house.

"Wait," said Holly in an odd voice. She pointed. At the far side of the lawn, five magpies strutted under the boughs of an old oak tree. The three kids watched in awe as the magpies poked around in the grass. "Five for silver," they whispered together.

They stood for several minutes, but the magpies ignored them and nothing happened.

The back of the house was more ordinary than the front but still imposing. The children clattered across a flagstoned yard and arrived at a small green door with a brass lion's-head knocker in the middle. Holly gave a loud rat-a-tat.

"Come in, come in. Nice to have young people visiting." Mr. Smythe waved them through the door and along a passage hung with coats and strewn with rubber boots and shoes. They stepped into a huge kitchen.

Despite his reluctance about the visit, Adam's eyes widened with pleasure. The room was like something in a museum, old fashioned and full of amazing junk. A large wooden table stood in the middle of the stone floor. At one end was a clear space where Mr. Smythe ate his meals. The rest of the table was covered with towers of books and magazines, bulging boxes, and, best of all, the sort of objects Adam wished his mom would let him keep.

A stuffed owl perched on a log anchored one pile of books; a glass case containing an old-fashioned collection of bird eggs topped another pile. A tray covered with a lineup of bones was balanced on top of several boxes. Stone Age axe heads and hammers held down sheets of paper covered with notes. A shallow plastic bowl full of sand held a small round urn partly glued together; the pieces still to be fitted rested on the sand's surface.

More books lined the shelves of an old dresser. They spilled over and marched in rows along the floor. Cracked jugs and strange iron objects hung from hooks in the ceiling. Stacks of old newspapers sat on every chair. Old photos, several showing aerial views of the White Horse, plastered the walls. A map acted as a window blind. The old-fashioned cookstove and much newer fridge looked out of place. This room was now an office, not a kitchen. In pride of place near the clear end of the table was a large white plastic skull with red glass eyes and a hole in the top, stuffed with pens and pencils.

"I gave him that last Christmas," whispered Owen when he saw Adam eyeing it. "It glows in the dark."

Mr. Smythe rubbed his hands together. "Brought something new to show me, did you?" His eyes twinkled at Owen and Adam. "An old talisman, I think you said?"

To Adam's relief Mr. Smythe made no mention of the fight.

"Actually, sir, I've got it." Holly handed over the piece of gold, with a sideways smirk at the two boys.

Owen rolled his eyes.

Mr. Smythe pushed aside a pile of papers and picked up a magnifying glass. "Make yourselves comfortable." He waved his hand towards the chairs, switched on a bright desk lamp and angled it on the talisman.

Holly and Owen each chose a chair, moved the contents from its seat to the floor and sat down, grinning. Adam copied them. Owen gave him a thumbs up.

"Most intriguing," muttered Mr. Smythe. His glasses began to slip down his nose. He grunted, pushed them up with one finger and continued his examination. "Hmm ... a spiral design on one side. Could be a decorative whirl, or the symbol for a snake, or a worm." He turned the talisman over. "Hmm, a horse. Possibly Celtic design." He placed it on a square of felt spread out on the tabletop, walked over to the dresser and pulled open a drawer. "Let's compare it to something." His hand paused in the air, then swooped down to pick out a small box. "This, I think, is the correct one." He removed the lid, gave a quick nod of satisfaction and returned to the table.

Placing the box on the table, Mr. Smythe removed the lid of a Chinese ginger jar, thrust his hand inside and pulled out a pair of thin white cotton gloves. He pulled them on before lifting a bronze coin from the box and placing it on the felt beside the gold talisman.

He beckoned to the children. "See the similarities?" he asked.

"They're nearly the same size and shape. They're both

old, and I think they've been made by hand because they're not perfect circles," Holly said. It was clear that she had worked with Mr. Smythe before.

"They both have designs of horses. Like the White Horse," offered Owen.

Adam decided it was time for him to get involved. "But one's gold and one's brown and they don't show the same horse, because this one —" Adam pointed to the bronze coin "— is only one horse, and this one —" he pointed to the magic talisman "— would show a large one and a small one if it was complete."

Mr. Smythe stared at him.

Adam flushed and avoided everyone's eyes. He must be more careful when he opened his big mouth.

Mr. Smythe held the talisman under the magnifying glass again. "You think this would show two Celtic horses," he muttered. "One large, one small. Could be. There is a suggestion of another leg on the edge of the break." He looked vaguely into the distance. "It reminds me of something ... now what?"

"Are there any lost horse carvings?" Holly asked. "Ones like the White Horse that have disappeared for some reason."

"Only the Red Horses of Tysoe," Mr. Smythe answered absently.

Holly, Owen, and Adam looked stunned, and Mr. Smythe sat up with a start. "That's it! That's what this reminds me of. Here." He gave the talisman back to Holly and dashed over to the dresser, where he started looking through the drawers.

Mr. Smythe rushed back to the table with a slim silver box in his hand.

Holly nudged Owen.

Mr. Smythe lifted the silver lid and took out an ancient, leather-bound volume. The book was fragile. Mr. Smythe laid it carefully on the felt, but as he opened it two of the thin pages fluttered out. Mr. Smythe sucked in his breath and carefully tucked them back in place. Then very slowly he turned the pages until he found the place he wanted. "There!"

The children gazed down at an old print of a landscape with the outline of two horses carved on a hill.

"The two red horses of Tysoe. Overgrown and lost in recent times. Now only known from this early sketch and a written description over three hundred years old." Mr. Smythe tapped the page with his forefinger. "When you asked about two horses, that's what it reminded me of." He fixed them all with a steely gaze. "Now come clean. What's all this about?"

CHAPTER NINE

A DASTARDLY DEED

Holly, Owen, and Adam exchanged swift glances.

"It's an odd story, sir," Owen said.

"And we can't tell you everything, because Chantel's not here," Holly added.

"Tell me what you can," said Mr. Smythe. "We've been friends since you were little tykes. Shared a lot of secrets."

"It began with Chantel," Owen said slowly. "We went to see her in the hospital. She showed us the talisman."

"Who gave it to her?" Mr. Smythe interjected.

Owen shrugged and spread his hands. "It was tucked in her hand when she came round from the anesthetic."

"Like a lucky charm," Holly added.

"But she woke up remembering a dream ..." Owen continued. He paused, searching for the right words.

Adam held his breath. Surely Owen wasn't going to tell about the White Horse.

"... that the talisman should be taken to Wayland's Smithy," Owen finished.

"So we did," Holly added.

Adam let out his breath. Owen and Holly were smart. They'd told nothing but the truth.

There was a long silence.

"Wayland's Smithy, eh?" Mr. Smythe grunted.

The three children nodded.

"And a coin-like talisman?"

The children nodded again.

Mr. Smythe fixed them with another steely glance. "You kids mixed up with horse magic?"

To his horror Adam started to laugh. He couldn't stop. It was all so ridiculous. The nervous laughter burst out of him and rang around the kitchen. "Horse magic ... is everyone in England nuts?" he sputtered.

No one smiled.

Owen kicked his ankle. "Shut up," he hissed.

Holly ignored them both.

Mr. Smythe stood up, walked over to the fridge and pulled out four cans of ginger beer. He offered one to Adam, then the others.

Adam grabbed it thankfully, opened the tab and took a long drink. He gave a small hiccup.

"Horse magic," mused Mr. Smythe, pouring his soda into a glass. "It's always been practiced in these parts." He leaned back and looked at the ceiling. "Of course, no one calls it that. The English government pays the National Trust to look after White Horse Hill. Scholars study the carving and discuss how it was made and used. Archeologists verify its age by 'optical dating.' But the local people do what they've always done — the ancient tradition of 'scouring' or cleaning the horse every seventh year. Interesting, eh?"

He took a drink from his glass. "Horses flourish in these vales. Ever wonder why?"

"Because of good grazing?" Holly offered.

"There are other good grazing areas in England," Mr. Smythe pointed out. "But this place has always been known for its racehorses. For thousands of years vale people have bred horses that are fleet of foot."

Mr. Smythe placed his ginger beer on the table and wandered over to a pile of books. He pulled one out, riffled through to the pages he wanted and passed the book to Adam.

Adam held it so Owen and Holly could see.

"St. George and the Dragon," Mr. Smythe said. "An old story from the vale."

"From Dragon Hill," Holly agreed.

"What's St. George riding?" Mr. Smythe asked Adam.

"A ... a ... white horse," Adam stammered, looking at the picture with new eyes.

"Exactly." Mr. Smythe jabbed the picture. "The horse, not St. George, fought the dragon. The monks added the saint to the story later."

Adam sucked in his breath.

Mr. Smythe swung round to Holly. "Ride a cock horse to Banbury Cross ... Finish the rhyme."

"To see a fine lady upon a white horse," Holly chanted, then stopped. "A white horse? That's horse magic too?"

Mr. Smythe sat down again, leaned back once again and stared upward. "Adults forget or ignore magical rhymes. But kids ... They're different." He seemed to be speaking to himself. "They have open minds. If I was the Great White Horse and wanted to make my presence known, I'd talk to a kid."

The three children stared at the floor.

"What about the dragon?" asked Adam eventually. "Why did the horse fight it?"

Holly and Owen looked at him curiously.

"Ah, the English dragons, sometimes referred to as worms. 'Worm Hill' and 'Wormley' are places where dragons lived." Mr. Smythe shook his head. "Dragons are nasty." He laughed. "Watch out for dragon talk. They twist words with a touch of honey to make them sound sweet!"

Adam squirmed. "Chinese dragons are lucky," he said. "The Chinese zodiac has a Year of the Dragon. We celebrate it in Canada. Last February, Chantel and I went to Chinese New Year in Edmonton. There was a big party in Chinatown with a dragon dance. It's lucky to be touched by the dragon, and it touched me and Chantel." He thought for a minute. "The Chinese people have a Year of the Horse too."

"The same symbols crop up in different cultures around the world," agreed Mr. Smythe, "but they are used in different ways. In England, the dragon is feared and not to be trusted."

Adam shifted on his chair.

Mr. Smythe continued, "Our dragon symbolizes things like hatred, fear, jealousy, and the dark side of human nature. During the last war, people said 'the dragon's stirring.'" He shrugged. "Maybe it was. In the stories, the dragon symbolizes evil and the White Horse symbolizes good."

"We've got to go," said Owen. "It's getting late. Thanks for the ginger beer." He stood up and put the pile of papers back on the seat of his chair.

Holly did the same, then paused for a moment. "Mr. Smythe," she said, "we can't say more right now, but can we come back?"

"Of course." Mr. Smythe escorted them to the back door. "Look after the talisman."

Holly patted her pocket.

He opened the door and they stepped out into the twilight.

"Don't mess with dragons," Mr. Smythe called after them. "But if one turns up, a personal sacrifice will give you power over it."

"What did he mean?" asked Adam after they'd waved a subdued goodbye and retraced their steps around the side of the house.

"Dunno. You tell us. You're the one who was asking about dragons," said Owen.

Adam lapsed into guilty silence again.

"Let's bring Chantel over tomorrow and tell Mr. Smythe everything," said Holly. "'Specially now that we know about the Tysoe horses. He'll help us find them. I know he will."

"The magpies were right," pondered Owen. "Five for silver. Mr. Smythe's book was in a silver box."

"Six for gold is next." Holly gave a little skip. "Maybe we'll find gold treasure and be rich, rich, rich!"

"Rich enough to fly to Disneyland," Owen fantasized.

"Rich enough to buy Disneyland," Adam countered.

They burst out laughing and walked back to the farm warbling, "When you wish upon a star ..."

Chantel was practicing on crutches. The evening was quiet and the hospital corridors free of traffic. All of a sudden she got the hang of it. She swung her cast and let the momentum move her body forward. Grinning, she flew down the corridor, bumping into a nurse who turned the corner unexpectedly.

"Goodness, Chantel. You've learned to move in a hurry. Be careful or you'll fall and be back in bed instead of going home tomorrow."

Chantel laughed and started back to her room.

"Bedtime," warned the nurse. "I'll be up with your last dose of medication when I've finished the patients at this end."

Chantel placed her crutches against her chair and eased herself into bed. She smiled. She was mobile again.

"Here you are." The nurse stuck two pills and a glass of water under Chantel's nose. Chantel swallowed, grimacing at the taste.

The nurse tucked her in. "Enjoy a good night's sleep and you'll be bright-eyed and bushy-tailed tomorrow. You're doing well, but another dull night in hospital won't hurt." She clicked off the overhead light and bustled out.

Chantel smiled. Dull nights? If the nurse only knew. She made herself comfortable, and closed her eyes.

Horse, are you there?

I'm here, child. Are you ready?

I'm ready. What are you going to show me this time?

Chantel wound her fingers through the silky mane, and sat confidently astride the Horse King's powerful back.

The last great celebration held on White Horse Hill. A fair called the Pastime held during my scouring.

What's a scouring?

When the villagers clean my carving so I shine for another seven years.

How long ago did this happen, Horse?

Time is different in my world. To me it is the blink of an eye. In your counting, the days of your great-grandparents' grandparents.

Chantel tried to work it out in years but failed. She gasped as the White Horse leapt for the stars. They sped through the evening, riding the warm summer breeze.

I need your help, little one. Our leap into the past will take all my magic, for I too will be seeing this for the first time.

What do you mean? asked Chantel.

The night before the Pastime, the red mare and I rode the wind together. Then she left for her scouring, and I for mine. Our bodies and the carving are one and the same during the scouring ceremony.

After I was cleaned, I rose again and rode the wind as usual, but the red mare never joined me. I never saw her again. Our time and your time are different. When I next came to her valley, many of your years had passed and the land had changed. I recognized nothing. I searched but there was no Magic Child to help. Now you have arrived. I will blend our magic together so we can both watch the Pastime and learn what happened.

What is my magic? What do I have to do? Chantel asked.

Just believe in me with all your heart.

I do. Chantel leaned forward and stroked his neck. *Oh horse, I do.* She sent a stream of love towards him.

They left the night far behind, and landed in brilliant sunshine beside the Ridgeway.

Watch, child. See through the eyes of Thomas, your ancestor.

🔲 🔲 🔲

Thomas Maxwell jiggled on the seat of the pony trap. His mother sighed and their groom stared straight ahead.

The day was hot and the Ridgeway crowded. People, horses, donkeys, and every kind of hand-pulled or horse-drawn vehicle were jammed together. The progress was slow ... oh so slow ... as they wound towards the giant earthworks at the top of White Horse Hill.

"Please hurry up. We'll miss the best part of the Pastime," Thomas fretted. He was hot and uncomfortable. He looked around for his Uffington friends, but there were too many people. Then he spotted Joe running through the crowds. He waved, but Joe didn't see him. Thomas sank back, wishing his mother would let him run on his own.

"This pony trap has the speed of a slug," he grumbled. Despite the tightness of his Sunday-best breeches, Thomas leapt off the carriage and ran alongside. He reached the pony and gave its rear a swat with the willow switch he was carrying.

"Nay, Master Thomas," said the groom "'Tis no use worriting the pony. The Ridgeway be fair choked with conveyances. We'd go no faster with a whole team of horses."

Thomas's shoulders slumped. This was the first year he'd been allowed to attend the Pastime, and they were going to miss all the best parts.

He walked beside the slow-moving carriage. "But I don't want to miss the jugglers, and the fire eater, and I want to buy one of Granny Bates' pies. They're the best. Everyone says so."

The groom laughed. "There be plenty of pies, and pig's ears, and cheese and ale. Thou will never starve, Master Thomas, as long as thy pockets be well lined."

Thomas drew a silver sixpence from his pocket and held it up proudly. "Look what Grandfather gave me."

"Thomas, put it away," said his mother sharply. "Pickpockets wander the crowds, not just jugglers and fire eaters." She rearranged her shawl around her shoulders.

The carriage lurched to a stop.

"Whatever's the matter now?" moaned Thomas's mother.

"There be a cart stuck in yon rut. No one will be passing till she be shifted." The groom left the carriage and went off to help.

Thomas's mother gave a deep sigh, closed her eyes and tilted her parasol to shade her face.

Thomas looked around. There was Joe again, with some friends. He took advantage of his mother's closed eyes to slip across the Ridgeway. He tugged Joe's sleeve. "What you doing, Joe?"

"Exploring. Want to come? We're going up the ramparts to watch from there."

"I'll ask." Thomas crossed his fingers and ran back to his mother. "Mama. Please may I go with the other boys?

Please, please! Georgie and Joe and Albert are here. We are going to scale the ditch and climb the ramparts so we can watch from there. I'll be careful. I promise. Please let me go." He held his crossed fingers behind his back and wished as hard as he could.

His mother glanced over at the waiting group and recognized them as fellow villagers. She looked around at the stalled carriages and nodded.

"Thank you, Mama! Thank you!" Thomas uncrossed his fingers and ran back to Joe.

His mother slumped back on the seat and closed her eyes.

"Quick, before she changes her mind," Thomas muttered. The small group of boys melted through the crowds and took off, sprinting over the fields.

They panted to a stop at the rim of the great ditch. Thomas eyed the steep sides with misgiving. Joe waved an imaginary sword over his head, gave a war whoop and plunged down into the ditch like a Saxon warrior. The other boys copied him.

Thomas manfully waved his willow switch and followed. He slipped and slid and felt the seam of his breeches give. But he didn't care. He was Thomas the Terrible invading Uffington Castle. He reached the bottom and looked up the steep grassy slope to the top of the ramparts. It was a long way up. Clenching his switch between his teeth, Thomas scaled the slope, hanging on to tufts of grass and sticking the tips of his shoes into any suggestion of a hollow.

His breath rasped in his throat. Dust stung his eyes and burrs and grass stains covered his breeches. He raised his eyes and gave a sigh of relief. He was within an arm's length of the top. But he had relaxed too soon. Without warning his foot slipped and he felt himself begin to slide backward.

"Help!" he yelled.

Joe's grinning face appeared over the edge. His arm shot out and grabbed Thomas by the collar of his shirt. He heaved. Thomas sputtered and coughed, as the neck of his shirt half choked him. Both boys sprawled on the grass.

Gasping, Thomas rolled over and thumped his thanks on Joe's back. They scrambled to their feet. The other boys were far ahead, yelling their excitement.

"'Tis a grand fair!" Thomas exclaimed. He could hardly begin to take in the amazing wonders spread below him. Booths filled the inner plateau. Flags fluttered and thin remnants of music floated through the air — flutes, whistles, panpipes, and the intermittent beating of the tabor.

"Look!" Thomas pointed to a stilt walker striding above the crowd and an organ grinder with a monkey collecting pennies in its cap. "I don't know what to watch first."

He goggled at a bear dancing around a stake, then laughed at a team of jugglers running through the crowd snatching parasols and kerchiefs from passersby and tossing them into the air.

"Come on, Tom. Let's see it all." Joe darted along the ramparts. Thomas followed.

"There are hundreds of carriages parked by the entrance," Thomas gasped. He had never seen so many vehicles in one spot.

His nose twitched. Enticing smells rose from nearby food booths. Warm pies and fresh bread, pork chitterlings and baked apples — the aromas made his mouth water. He sniffed hungrily. "I bet those are Granny Bates' pies," he said. "Come on, Joe. I'll buy you one."

They slid down the bank on the seats of their pants and darted into the crowd. The two boys dodged past people in their Sunday best, tripped over a pair of fighting dogs and followed their noses to the pie booth.

"Two pies, please." Thomas proudly held out his sixpence.

He sank his teeth into the fragrant pastry. Hot gravy burnt his lips and ran down his chin, but it was delicious. "Mmmm, steak, kidney and mushroom. Mother should hire Granny Bates as our cook," he mumbled. "This is better than anything our housekeeper makes."

"Come and see the scouring," said Joe, his voice muffled by pie. Pastry flakes covered his chest.

Thomas laughed and looked down at his own clothes. Spots of gravy and a thousand crumbs joined the grass stains and burrs. His mother would have a fit when she saw him again, so he might as well make his adventure a good one.

He followed Joe back up the ramparts.

The downs fell away to the valley as usual, but today the White Horse could hardly be seen. The carving was covered with hundreds of men. Some were on their hands and knees scraping away the top layer of chalk. Others were trimming the edges of the figure with sharp knives. Still more men toiled uphill from a nearby quarry, carrying buckets of fresh white chalk. This was poured on the cleaned areas and tamped into place with stout poles. The empty buckets were filled with the scrapings and taken back downhill. The work was done in respectful silence.

Thomas watched in fascination. "Is your father helping?"

"'Course he is," said Joe proudly. "He's been scouring since his fourteenth birthday. I'll do the same."

"Me too." Thomas straightened his back. "I'm seven now, but I'll be fourteen next scouring."

Joe drew himself up taller. "When Pa's dead I'll take over his job like he did from Grandpapa. I'll be the next Eye Maker," he boasted.

Thomas hesitated. He didn't want to seem ignorant, but his mother had not told him much about the scouring. "What's that?"

"He's the man who scrapes the eye clean. It's the most important job of the scouring," said Joe. "It's done first. Pa did it yesterday. He collects the eye scrapings in a bucket and mixes them with some fresh chalk. He has to ride with the bucket to the Vale of the Red Horse. The red mare is being scoured too. Pa stamps his scrapings into the eye socket of the red mare. He stays overnight and rides back here for the end of our scouring festivities. He'll be back this afternoon."

The booming call of the Blowing Stone sounded from the far side of the earthworks. People obeyed the call, streaming out to stand along the edge of the slope into the Manger.

"Come on, Thomas. That's the signal for the first race." Joe started to run. "They're going to chase the cheese down the Manger."

"Wait for me!" Thomas struggled to keep up. He made it through the ditch in one piece, then crawled on his hands and knees through the legs of the crowd to sit beside Joe on the very edge of the Manger.

Fourteen stalwart young men stood flexing their muscles at the head of the steep drop.

Thomas gasped. "They're never going to run down there, are they?"

"They are." Joe grinned. "Pa said they ran horses down in the old days. But I don't believe that."

"Me neither!" Thomas's eyes were as round as Granny Bates' pies.

A bear of a man, wearing the striped apron of a butcher, rolled a large wheel of cheese to the head of the Manger. The contestants readied themselves in a ragged line behind it. The chairman of the games appeared, riding a white horse. He reined in and held out a red handkerchief.

"Cheese!" hollered the chairman.

The butcher pushed the cheese wheel over the edge of the slope. It bounced from hillock to hillock in gigantic leaps.

"Go!" the chairman shouted as he dropped the red hand-kerchief.

The lads leapt forward.

Some lost their footing right away, rolling and sliding down the steep slope. Others tottered and stumbled, out of control. The race was between two young men who threw their bodies well back, dug in their heels at every step and kept their balance. One was a fair-haired lad from Wantage and the other a dark-haired gypsy.

Thomas hooted and hollered. "I bet the gypsy wins, don't you, Joe?"

"Naw. Look at the legs on that Wantage lad. They're strong as tree trunks."

The crowd egged the pair on and the race looked like a dead heat until they reached the bottom. Then the gypsy showed his speed. He sped like a racehorse to the cheese, touching it a full body length ahead of his rival.

The Blowing Stone sounded again, louder and more urgent. It blew and blew, the sound booming around the vale.

The startled crowd moved back into the earthworks to see what was happening.

Thomas felt brave now. He pushed and wriggled as well as Joe. He elbowed through legs and slipped between voluminous skirts until he found himself at the center of the fair, pressed up against the stage built for the wrestling.

Two men stood on the stage.

"'Tis Pa." Joe sounded startled. "He looks right upset. Something must be wrong." He waved to attract his father's attention, but his father did not look down.

"Who's the other man?" asked Thomas.

"The town crier from Wantage," Joe replied.

The town crier rang his hand bell. "Hear ye! Hear ye!" he bellowed.

The music stopped. The crowd fell silent.

"Hear ye the words of the Eye Maker. Take note, for the news be dreadful."

Joe's father took a deep breath, stepped forward and shouted as loudly as he could, "Dear friends and neighbors, I have just returned from the Vale of the Red Horse. Sadly ... the red mare is no more."

A gasp rose from the audience. They strained to hear more.

"The landowner refused to do his duty," Joe's father continued. "He would not give the gold to supply the scourers with their bread and ale."

A scatter of boos sounded, and silence fell.

Joe's father swallowed hard. "The scourers ... they pro-tested ... but the landowner grew angry. Last night ... he harnessed his horses ... and ploughed the red mare under." His voice cracked. "Her like will ne'er be seen again."

Sadness and shock rippled through the crowd. Hand-kerchiefs fluttered as some of the ladies wiped their eyes. But the shocked silence prevailed. The crowd was waiting.

"Is the same thing going to happen to our horse?" Thomas whispered.

Joe trod on his foot. "Shhhh, listen."

"Hear ye! Hear ye!" the town crier bellowed once more. "Lord Craven-Smythe, who willingly supplies the bread and ale for our scouring, has made a decree. Let it be known that he will seek help from the government of this fair land. He will ask the House of Lords to pass laws to preserve our ancient White Horse forever."

The Blowing Stone's note echoed again and again as the crowd roared its approval and broke into spontaneous song.

> "We'll glorify the king.
> We'll glorify the king.
> We'll leap the downs, and ride the wind,
> And glorify the king."

Thomas and Joe stood in the center of the crowd.

"The poor red mare. That's not right," said Thomas. "Someone should make her again. Come on, Joe. Help me wish. Let's do horse magic."

The two boys faced each other and linked the little fin-gers of their right hands. They closed their eyes and chanted,

"We wish, we wish, but ne'er in vain. We wish the red mare back again." They unclasped their little fingers, held them up and spat over them.

The vision shimmered and faded.

Chantel sniffed, her eyes full of tears. *The red mare was ploughed under. That's why she never came back. How awful.* She wiped her eyes and sniffed again.

Equus whickered softly. *But you are the Magic Child. You will raise her for me. You will make Thomas's wish come true.*

Was Thomas really my ancestor?

He was.

Wow. I'm glad I liked him.

Equus gave a bray of laughter. *You now have all the information I can give you, child. The blacksmith will assist. Sleep deeply and believe. I will watch and wait.*

Chantel threw her arms around his neck and hugged as tightly as she could. *I'm glad you were saved forever.*

She wanted to say more, but the dream had tired her out. Her eyelids drooped. She let sleep take over.

CHAPTER TEN

THAT YOU MUST NOT SEEK

Back at White Horse Farm, Owen slept, but Adam forced himself to stay awake. He needed the half-talisman so he could visit the dragon again. He wanted to ask the dragon to help him find the red mare. If they found the red mare, they would find the other half of the talisman. If they found the other half of the talisman, he could free the dragon and share its power. Adam couldn't stop thinking about how the dragon's power might make his life better.

The problem was, he didn't have the broken talisman. He had tried a million excuses to borrow it from Holly, but she wouldn't let him.

"Go away. It's my turn," she'd said, laughing.

Adam had tried sneaking the gold piece out of her jeans pocket while she was in the bath, but Auntie Lynne had chased him from the girls' room before he'd found it. He was desperate. There was only one way left. He'd wait until everyone was asleep, then snitch it.

If the dragon could find the red mare, why didn't the White Horse ask him to help? said a small voice at the back of his mind.

Adam groaned silently. There was his conscience again, making life difficult. Like Mr. Smythe, it kept telling him the dragon was bad news. He suppressed the annoying voice. The dragon was nice. He would help it, and it would help him. He just needed the half-talisman!

He crept to the bedroom door, cracked it open and checked who was asleep. The light was out in Holly's room. Auntie Lynne had gone to bed early and her room was dark. But he could hear the TV. Uncle Ron was still downstairs.

Adam returned to bed, his mind drifting back to the meeting with Mr. Smythe. Adam had never met an adult like him. A historian who believed in horse magic and dragon magic. Amazing!

Do you believe in magic? asked his conscience.

Adam stared at the shaft of moonlight banding the covers on his bunk. He considered the question and spoke softly to himself. "I guess I do now. I believe in horse magic and dragon magic."

A feeling of warmth and friendship washed over him.

Hello, Adam, said a kindly voice inside his head. I knew you would become a believer. I'm the White Horse. Now you can call for me whenever you need me. Remember ... I am always here.

Adam froze, not daring to reply. This was too much ...

another voice. No way was he getting involved with that horse ... it was hard enough dealing with the dragon. Terrified, he curled into a ball and waited and waited until the feeling of friendship faded away.

⊠ ⊠ ⊠

"The brother admits he believes in me!" rejoiced Equus. "The others will follow, I know it. They believe in their hearts. They just have to declare."

"But the brother is still influenced by the dragon," worried Myrddin.

"He is, but have faith. If he chooses us of his own free will, our magic will grow a hundredfold," Equus replied.

Myrddin twitched his cloak. "The dragon offers power and flattery."

"The boy heard Equus. He is beginning to listen to his heart," Ava said.

Myrddin shook his head. "It seems so futile. Still only two, at the most four, human children."

Ava gave a ripple of laughter. "How soon you forget, Myrddin. Remember watching helplessly from the stars? That was futile. Now we have hope!"

She spread her wings and soared around her companions. "Celebrate the hope. Hope the human children will find the red mare. Hope they will restore the talisman. A human shattered the talisman. If a human causes it to be remade, Equus will be whole again." Ava gave a shrill echoing call. "Myrddin, maybe the children will help you and me. Celebrate the hope. Celebrate the hope!"

It was midnight. Adam lay rigid in his bunk. The White Horse had not spoken again. Maybe he had dreamed it. His conscience was quiet now too, and so was the dragon. The only sounds now were those of the old farmhouse settling for the night. His eyelids drooped for the hundredth time. He shook himself awake.

Uncle Ron finished watching TV. Adam heard his heavy footsteps creaking up the stairs and along the corridor. Adam checked his luminous watch dial. How long should he give Uncle Ron, ten minutes, half an hour, an hour? Not an hour. He couldn't stay awake that long.

He turned over and watched the chink of moonlight creep across the floorboards. He'd get up when it reached ... His eyes closed again.

Adam pulled himself up with a start. If he was going to search Holly's room, it was now or never. He wriggled out of his bunk bed. One of Owen's arms hung loosely over the side, but Adam slipped past it. He tiptoed to the door. Owen stirred slightly. Adam stiffened, then relaxed. If anyone challenged him, he was just going to the bathroom. He lifted the latch on the door and tiptoed into the corridor.

The boards under his feet squeaked and groaned no matter how quiet he tried to be. He reached the bathroom door, opened it and flicked on the light. All was silent except for the beating of his heart and a faint rumble from his aunt and uncle's room. He grinned. Uncle Ron was snoring. Good.

Adam stepped across the corridor to the girls' room.

The door squeaked as it opened, but again no one stirred. He slipped inside.

Using the beam of light spilling from the bathroom, Adam tried to find Holly's jeans in the piles of clothes scattered on the floor. First he found her T-shirt, then a sweater. Ah ... his toes felt tough jean material. He squatted on the floor and felt up each leg and into every pocket. The talisman wasn't there.

Adam groaned silently. He could guess where it was; Holly was sleeping with it. He peered through the dim light towards Holly's bed and realized only then that something was wrong. The room was too quiet. No one was breathing there but him.

He padded over to the bed and felt the covers.

The bed was empty. Holly wasn't there.

Owen woke up terrified. A hand was clamped over his mouth, and another hand shook his shoulder.

"Owen, wake up," a voice whispered. "Wake up ... but be quiet."

The hand tightened over Owen's mouth as he groaned.

"It's me, Adam," the whisper continued. "Nod your head if you're awake."

Owen nodded frantically.

The hand removed itself from his mouth.

"Wha ... what the heck?" Owen sputtered. "Idiot. You nearly smothered me."

"Shhhhhh! I'm sorry. I was scared you'd yell and wake

the whole house," Adam whispered. "You've got to come with me. Holly's missing and I bet I know where she's gone ... to Dragon Hill."

"You're dreaming, Adam. Go back to bed."

"I'm not, I'm not." Adam shook Owen's shoulder again. "The dragon took me there the night I slept with the talisman. Now he's taken Holly."

Owen stared blearily at Adam. "You met a dragon? You never said. When?"

Adam ignored the question. "Look, if you don't believe me, go and check Holly's room. She's not there. She's not in the house. I bet she fell asleep holding the talisman and the dragon took her to Dragon Hill. That's what happened to me. Come on, Owen! We've gotta follow her and see what she's up to. I've tried, but there's no way I can find my way to Dragon Hill in the dark."

Still muddled with sleep, Owen swung himself out of bed, switched on the light and stared at his cousin. Adam was dressed in his jacket and boots. He was smeared with mud and looked exhausted.

"Why should I help you? You want to talk to a dragon in the middle of the night, go right ahead." Owen turned to climb back into his bunk.

"I can't find my way in the dark," cried Adam in frustration. He thought fast. "What if Holly needs help? Mr. Smythe said dragons are trouble."

"If this is for real, you've got some explaining to do, Adam Maxwell," said Owen. He dressed silently.

The night was black. Clouds obscured the moon and stars. Owen knew the way well, but the darkened land looked unfamiliar. Tree branches grabbed the boys from above, and grasses and weeds snatched at their pant legs below.

Adam was scared, but anger drove him on. He would have done anything rather than wake Owen, but there was no other way of getting to Dragon Hill. His anger at Holly burned deep inside him and fueled his determination to find out what was going on. And now he couldn't even trust the dragon. How dare the dragon talk to Holly instead of him, Adam? He was the dragon's friend.

The boys stumbled across country to avoid going past prying eyes in the village. Eventually, scratched and winded, they reached the lane that wound towards Dragon Hill.

They stopped to catch their breath.

"We're going to look right idiots if she's not up there," said Owen.

"She will be ... I know it," panted Adam. He peered through the night, trying to make out the top of Dragon Hill. "See ... I'm right! There's a glow ... on the top."

Owen could see nothing.

"You owe me, Adam Maxwell," Owen grumbled as he set off up the lane. "You owe me big time."

They trudged on in silence until they came to the foot of Dragon Hill. Adam clutched Owen's arm and pointed again. This time the glow of light at the top of the hill was unmistakable, but what worried Adam was that unlike the soft glow from the talisman, this glow was blood red.

"Don't make a sound as we climb up," Adam whispered. "Crawl the last bit. Until we can see what's going on."

Owen grunted agreement and they started the climb.

A rough stairway was gouged into the side of the hill. But the turf steps were damp and slippery. Both boys found it safer to half crawl. They clambered slowly and silently.

Nausea gripped Adam as he climbed upward. His head began to throb and the anger gnawed at his stomach. How dare Holly take his talisman and meet with the dragon? The dragon was his. He needed its power; Holly didn't. With each step upward, his emotions grew stronger, until Adam was trembling.

They heard voices.

"No!" Holly's clear tones carried though the night. "I won't say the words."

Owen unexpectedly touched Adam's arm. Adam jumped and swung around, his fist clenched, ready to fight. Owen backed off, his face puzzled and uneasy in the red glow. "Is she talking to the dragon?" he whispered.

Adam dropped his fist and nodded. Both boys began to wriggle on their bellies up the last part of the slope.

"Say the words of power, and I'll fly you home," they heard the dragon wheedle in a voice that dripped honey. "We could fly anywhere. What great wonders would you like to see?"

Adam was furious. The dragon was offering Holly the same things he'd offered Adam.

Holly's voice rang out, "Listen, bonehead, all I want to see is my bed."

"Uh-oh," whispered Owen. "She's furious. I wonder why she's not stomped off. That's what she usually does when she's mad."

Adam barely heard. He concentrated on raising his head until he could see across the flat top of Dragon Hill. The small plateau was bathed in a red glow from what had been the bald spot on the ground. Now it was a pulsing, transparent membrane covering a hole filled with fiery red light. Holly, in her pajamas, was standing on the far side, facing them. Her arms were folded defiantly across her chest, and her chin jutted.

"Why doesn't she run away?" Owen whispered. He shuddered.

Adam stared across at Holly. "Shut up and listen."

"Don't you like power?" The dragon's voice oozed enticingly. "Think what you could do with the power, if you and I were partners."

"Power! Is that what you offered Adam?" Holly blurted out. "He'd like that. He's feeling pretty awful right now with his mum and dad splitting up and Chantel in the hospital. You would! Just like the fairy stories. Find the weak person and offer them power. Huh!" She gave an angry laugh. "You got me instead!"

Adam drew in a sharp breath, as though he'd been kicked in the stomach. How could Holly say he was weak? How dare she talk about his parents divorcing? What did she know, anyway?

A scaly tail swirled under the surface of the membrane. "You're angry. That makes you more powerful," hissed the dragon. "Though your anger is not as good as the boy's. His anger almost fills his being. When he held the talisman I could feel his rage. As it grew so did my power." The dragon laughed, and the membrane glowed a deeper red. "I feel it even now. The boy's anger is so strong, it's as though he were right here." The dragon laughed again. "He feeds me."

Holly stamped the ground. "You make Adam angry so you can use him? That's horrible."

At the rim of the plateau, Owen turned to stare at Adam.

Adam's face burned with humiliation. He felt betrayed. The dragon wasn't his friend; he was using him.

"The boy was nothing, just a passing human whose anger helps me grow strong. But you ... you're different. You are a very clever girl. Sometimes it's hard for clever girls to gain power." The dragon's voice grew sweeter with every word. "But I could change all that. Imagine having all the power you need, everything you want within your grasp, everyone at your command. That's what you and I could achieve together. The talisman is the key. Now I am stronger, I need not wait for the other half. Hold it and say the words of power. And I will give you your heart's desire."

Holly ignored him.

Adam stared through the dark, trying to read Holly's face. He knew what was happening. She was considering the dragon's offer. She was going to say the words of power. Once again, he would lose out! He could contain himself no longer. Erupting onto the plateau, he yelled at the top of his voice, "What about your promise to me, Worm? It's me who needs the power, so I can fix things! You promised!"

The dragon heaved under the membrane and showed a flash of teeth. "So I *could* feel your presence," the dragon hissed. "You were hiding on the hill. Why?"

"Adam!" Holly cried. "Don't talk to him. He's a dragon. He lies. That's what dragons do."

The dragon sweetened his voice again. "So you've come

to help me, Adam. That's good. I missed you. I'm sorry. I thought you had changed your mind and given the talisman away. I'm glad you came after it. You can say the words of power instead of this silly wench. She's only a girl. She doesn't understand."

Adam paused uncertainly.

"Chauvinist pig," said Holly coldly. "It's you that doesn't understand. I have the talisman, remember?" She held it up. The light behind the membrane dimmed.

Only Owen noticed.

"Put it away!" cried the dragon with a roar. "I don't need to see it ... I need you to hold it and say the words of power. Quickly! Then we can all have what we desire." The membrane stretched upward as a claw thrust against it.

"Forget it," Holly retorted. "Adam, listen to him lie. That big red lump's never going to let a kid share his power."

"Silence," roared the dragon. "Children should respect their elders."

"What century are you from?" retorted Holly.

The dragon's voice sank to a musical whisper. "See, Adam? The girl doesn't understand, but you do. You realize what power can do. She doesn't even want power. I know what she'd like, though. Give the talisman to Adam, girl, then choose your reward. The jewels of a princess, servants, velvet dresses? Anything. Then we can all have what we wish."

Holly burst out laughing. "You're so retro!" she sputtered.

Adam stared at her. He never understood girls. How could she laugh? He looked down through the membrane. The dragon stared up at him and grinned.

Feelings slid out of the red pit and wrapped around him.

Adam shivered. They were nothing like the feeling of friendship from the horse, or the magic from Wayland's Smithy. The overpowering feeling here was hate. Horrified, he stepped back, but it was too late. He had looked into the dragon's eyes.

"Don't go, Adam. You can help me," whispered the dragon. His hypnotic voice filled Adam's head and the hatred filled his body. "Take the talisman from the girl. You don't need her. She's like the others; she'll stop you doing what you want. Take the talisman. She cannot run away. I've put a barrier spell around her. Take the talisman. Take it. Take it! I'll teach you the words of power. You and I will do everything we planned."

The words became a drumbeat in Adam's head. "Take it! Take it! Take it!" His feet turned and marched him around the pit towards Holly.

White-faced, Holly watched his approach. She tried to step back, but the invisible barrier stopped her. She clenched her fist and placed it protectively behind her back.

Adam stopped in front of her. "Give me the talisman," he said. His voice was empty and his eyes blank.

Holly shook her head

"Give me the talisman." Adam's lips moved, but his voice was the voice of the dragon.

Holly froze with terror. She stared mutely back.

"I will destroy you!" The dragon's voice screamed out of Adam's mouth as Adam's hand penetrated the invisible barrier.

Against her will, Holly felt her hand move towards Adam's.

As their fingers met, out of the darkness leapt Owen, weirdly dancing and singing around the membrane.

"Nobody likes me, everybody hates me, think I'll go and

eat worms ..." he sang, his voice becoming a shout. "Get it, you creep ... WORMS!"

Adam's hand stopped. A flicker of life returned to his blank eyes as he heard Owen's voice. A look of horror crossed his face. He snatched his hand back through the barrier. "No!" he shrieked. "You can't make me do things." He fainted.

A roar of anger rose from the pit.

Owen danced frantically past Holly. "Use the talisman. The worm's scared of it," he whispered. "Call the White Horse." He waved his arms and did silly movements with his legs, then danced away, singing at the top of his voice, "Big fat chewy ones, icky slimy gooey ones ..."

"WHO are yoooou?" roared the dragon. The red membrane heaved and shuddered as he tried to keep track of Owen's movements.

At Holly's feet Adam stirred. "Yes," he whispered. "Call the horse ... sacrifice the talisman. Mr. Smythe said ... throw it away."

Stubbornly Holly shook her head. "The dragon will get it."

"See how they wriggle and squirm ... you worm!" yelled Owen. He danced past Holly again. "Call, you idiot," he hissed.

"Call the horse. I'll help," Adam muttered groggily. He struggled to stand.

"Bite off their heads, and suck out the juice, and throw the skins away," roared Owen around the edge of the membrane. His gyrations grew more ridiculous. "Nobody knows how I exist ..."

Adam turned his face towards White Horse Hill. "White Horse," he croaked. He turned to Holly. "Help," he said. Tears were running down his cheek. "Sacrifice the talisman."

Holly looked at the pit, at Owen's gyrating figure and back at Adam's desperate face. She gave a little nod and held the talisman high. "White Horse, help!" she yelled, and tossed the talisman in the air.

Brilliant light surrounded them, illuminating a great white stallion who reared over the pulsing red membrane with flailing hooves.

"NOOOOOOoooooooo!" roared the dragon as the membrane split.

A column of fire shot into the sky.

The ground shuddered as the hooves pounded and smashed, the claws and teeth ripped and snapped. The whirling white light and red fire spiraled up to the sky, growing so intense the children covered their eyes.

Everything went black.

The silence was total.

The dragon and horse were gone.

"Owen? Adam? Is anyone there? Please be there." Holly's voice trembled.

"I'm here, Holly. It's so dark I daren't move. I'm scared of falling in the dragon's pit," Owen answered. "Adam, are you there?"

"I ... I'm here ... I just can't see." Adam's voice shook.

Gradually their eyes adjusted and the dark became less dense. The three cousins could pick out each other's silhouettes against the sky.

"I still can't see what's in the middle of the plateau," Owen shouted to Adam and Holly. "Stay put. I'll walk around the edge."

Adam stretched out his hand towards Holly. "I'm so sorry, I'm sorry. I didn't mean ... It wasn't me. It was the dragon.

He was inside me saying and doing things. It wasn't me!"

Holly grasped his hand tightly. "I know. It's okay."

They watched as Owen walked around the circle to join them.

All three hugged.

"Has the dragon been destroyed for good?" Holly asked.

"Dunno," said Adam. "He just went up in the sky."

"So did the horse. Did you see the white light? It sort of spiraled around the red fire and wrapped it up. It was brilliant," said Owen.

"Let's go home," Holly sniffed. "I hate this place."

They helped each other inch backward down the steep slope.

"I didn't shake when I was arguing with the dragon," Holly said between chattering teeth. "Don't know why I'm doing it now."

"Shock. That's what you told me after Chantel's accident," Adam said.

The children supported each other. Together they stumbled down the lane as the clouds parted and a fitful moon gave enough light to show their way.

Adam looked across Holly to Owen. His teeth gleamed as he gave a crooked grin.

"Think I'll go and eat worms! Was that the best distraction you could think of?"

"Worked, didn't it?" retorted Owen.

Three sets of shoulders shook, this time with giggles.

The giggles grew into chuckles and the chuckles to gales of healing laughter. The laughter rose in the air and was swept by a breeze to circle the stars.

"You and the children prevailed?" asked Ava.

"This time," replied Equus wearily. The half-talisman on his forelock gleamed dully. "But my talisman must be made whole. The dragon grows in strength."

Myrddin nodded. "Does the dragon know the Dark Being is approaching?"

Equus shook his head. "Not yet. He recognized only the stirring caused by the Magic Child, and his ability to feed on anger. But there is no way of preventing his further increase of power. Soon he will recognize the truth."

"He is gone from Dragon Hill?" asked Ava.

"Yes," replied Equus. "I cannot strengthen earth bonds until the talisman is whole. Dragon Hill can no longer contain him. I used star bonds as confinement. But he and I will clash again."

Myrddin sadly nodded agreement.

"Return the talisman to the Magic Child, Equus. Hope she and her cousins can renew it before your next struggle." Ava gave a shiver. "Other supporters from the dark side are beginning to stir. I feel them. I wish the Lady was awake to guide us."

"Soon," said Myrddin. He and Ava held out their arms beseechingly and called across the sky, "Traa dy liooar?"

Equus leapt once more through time and space. He dropped the talisman on Chantel's pillow without waking her and returned to the stars.

CHAPTER ELEVEN

TOGETHER AGAIN

Owen, Holly, and Adam slept late the next morning.

Holly was first up. Grabbing a banana from the kitchen, she sat on the paddock wall and let the sunshine chase away the dark dreams. Owen joined her, hair rumpled and eyes bleary.

"You look terrible," Holly said. She offered a bite of banana.

Owen pushed it away. "You wouldn't win a beauty pageant either." He sat beside her. "Did you see Mum's note?"

Holly shook her head.

"She's gone to the city to fetch Chantel. Where's Dad?"

Holly waved her arm. "Around. He and Mr. O'Reilly are waiting for a buyer. There's been an uproar in the village, though."

"Oh. What's up?" asked Owen without much interest. He leaned against the gatepost and lifted his face to the sun.

Holly looked sideways at her brother. "Some vandals set

a fire on Dragon Hill. All the grass is burnt and everyone is up in arms because the downs could have caught alight. The police are checking it out for clues."

Owen's eyes snapped wide open and he sat up so fast he nearly fell off the wall. "What?"

Holly chuckled. "I made up the last bit. No police. At least, not that I've heard."

"Jeez ... What a crazy night!" Owen glanced at his sister. "How are you feeling?"

"I'm fine ... it seems unreal. If Mr. O'Reilly hadn't mentioned the fire, I'd have thought it was a dream."

The family station wagon drove into the farmyard. Chantel leaned out of the window, waving frantically. Adam appeared from the kitchen, and Uncle Ron ran out from the barn. Everyone converged on the wagon, offering help.

"No thanks. I can do it myself. See?" Chantel eased herself up on her crutches and swung her leg forward. "I can even go fast."

"No you don't, young lady." Auntie Lynne caught her by the waist. "Not on these cobbles. We don't want to risk another fall."

Chantel laughed up at her. "I promise I'll go slow on the cobbles." She crossed carefully to the farmhouse door and looked back in triumph.

"You're a regular little Hopalong," Uncle Ron winked. "Don't overdo it. Rest when you're tired. Glad you're back, Shrimp, but I've got someone waiting to see me." He headed back to the barn.

Auntie Lynne followed everyone into the kitchen. "If you kids are happy entertaining Chantel, I'll catch up on the accounts. Call if you need anything." She drifted upstairs.

Everyone waited until her footsteps were heard overhead, then started talking at once.

"I had another dream," said Chantel.

"Wait till you hear what happened to me," Holly said.

"Last night was amazing," said Owen.

"We had a fight with a dragon," said Adam.

"Stop!" yelled Chantel, and put her hands over her ears. Everyone laughed.

Holly dropped her voice. "We shouldn't talk here. Mum and Dad might hear."

"Let's go to the stable," suggested Owen.

"Mr. O'Reilly's there. Let's take Chantel to meet Mr. Smythe. He needs to hear everything anyway," said Holly.

Chantel pulled a face. "We're telling an adult?"

"He's helping us," Holly explained. "He knows about horse magic. And he knows about the lost red horses."

Chantel sat up sharply. "He does? Mr. Smythe knows where to find the red mare?"

"Yes," chorused three voices.

"Let's go." Chantel reached for her crutches.

"We'll phone first. He might be busy." Owen picked up the mobile phone and wandered out into the sunshine, dialing. Holly ran after him, leaving Chantel and Adam alone.

"Er ... I'm glad you're home," Adam said, not meeting her eyes.

Chantel beamed. "Really?"

Adam flushed but nodded.

Chantel waved a crutch. "You can try these if you like. They're fun."

Adam gave a strained smile. "Mom and Dad phoned you, didn't they?" he said.

"Yes ... I don't remember much. My head hurt."

Adam chose his words carefully. "So you don't remember how they were?"

"You mean, if they were fighting again?" said Chantel sadly.

"You know about the fighting?" Adam asked, astonished.

"I'm not a baby. 'Course I know." Chantel's lip trembled. "No one wants me around. They're too busy fighting and you're too mad at everything. So sure I know." Her face softened. "But I've a friend here. The White Horse wants me."

"Hey, I'm your brother!"

"But you're always mad at me."

Adam shrugged and looked ashamed. "Because you're the youngest and never in trouble. Mom and Dad like you best."

"They don't." Chantel's eyes flashed. "They like you best because you're a boy and the oldest. You get to do everything and I'm always left out."

Brother and sister glared at each other.

"Will they get a divorce?" Chantel suddenly asked.

"They might," said Adam.

"What will happen to us?" Chantel's eyes watered.

Adam shrugged. "Live with Mom and visit Dad at weekends, I guess. That's what my friend Jason does."

Chantel's face was white. She seemed tiny and frail.

"No matter what happens to Mom and Dad, we're still together," Adam said awkwardly.

Chantel struggled to smile. "Okay."

A Land Rover drew up in front of White Horse Farm, driven by Mr. Smythe. He stowed Chantel in the front seat beside a pile of old books. Owen, Holly, and Adam scrambled into the back.

"It's a beautiful day." Mr. Smythe rubbed his hands together. "We'll start at the White Horse. Seems a good place to listen to your story." He circled the farmyard, saluting Uncle Ron as they passed the barn.

"The White Horse will like that," said Chantel softly.

They drove sedately through the village and roared up the lane past Dragon Hill.

"Dragon Hill is so close in a car," whispered Holly. "It seemed miles away last night."

Mr. Smythe parked at the viewpoint, and they all got out of the car. The carving of the White Horse flowed away from them over the curve of the hill, but its face and eye could clearly be seen staring up at the sky. The blackened top of Dragon Hill stared up from the valley below.

Mr. Smythe gestured towards it. "I suppose you lot had something to do with that," he commented.

Holly, Adam, and Owen looked uncomfortable.

"It wasn't our fault. Promise not to tell," begged Holly.

"A good officer never jumps to conclusions until he's heard the full account," Mr. Smythe hedged. He set up a folding chair for Chantel.

Everyone else sprawled on the warm grass.

Owen stared at the carved face. "The horse seems different, more alive. Does it see and hear everything, Chantel?"

Chantel thought for a moment. "I wouldn't say anything nasty about him." She grinned. "He'd hear that for sure."

Everyone started talking at once.

"One at a time, one at a time," Mr. Smythe protested. "It's too complicated to work out unless I hear one story at a time. Who's first?"

"Chantel," the older cousins chorused.

"Fine." Mr. Smythe settled himself on his back with a grass blade in his mouth.

Once more Chantel told her story.

Next, Adam explained about the talisman, the dragon dream, and Wayland's Smithy. This time he told the whole truth.

Everyone listened intently.

"So that's how you knew what had happened to Holly when she disappeared from her bed," commented Owen.

Finally Holly told about the uproar on Dragon Hill, how Owen had distracted the dragon, Adam had suggested sacrificing the talisman, and the White Horse had come to their rescue.

"So ... what do you think, Mr. Smythe?" asked Owen. "Weird, isn't it? But you do believe us, don't you?"

The four children gazed anxiously at the historian.

"I'm envious," Mr. Smythe said slowly. "I wish I had the eyes and mind of a child to enjoy such a brilliant adventure."

"Er ... is that a yes or no, sir?" Adam prompted.

Mr. Smythe spread his hands. "So help me, I'm a trained historian. Historians demand proof." He pointed to Dragon Hill. "There's proof someone was fooling around with fire, but it doesn't prove the events of your exciting night."

The children's shoulders slumped.

"I've seen the talisman," continued Mr. Smythe. "Most intriguing, but tests and research can't prove magic." He shrugged. "Pity it's gone."

He gestured towards the Ridgeway. "I've walked to Wayland's Smithy many times. But Wayland has never spoken to me." He patted Chantel's hand. "Both of Chantel's dreams described many things I knew and much I didn't. Most facts will be impossible to check." He gazed around at the disappointed faces. "Proof of your dreams and adventures is impossible ... but ... I believe you," he finished.

"Hooray," shouted Holly and Owen.

"Yes!" said Adam.

Chantel beamed. "Then I'll tell you about my last dream."

"You've had another? You didn't say." Adam huffed. "How come?"

"You were so full of the dragon adventure. Besides ..." Chantel hesitated and gave an apologetic glance at Mr. Smythe. "I wanted to meet Mr. Smythe before I said anything." Her voice dropped. "I don't want you to think I've still got concussion and should go back to the hospital."

"I certainly don't think that, young lady," Mr. Smythe reassured her. "Whatever else your dreams are, they are not nonsense." He lay on his back again. "Fire away."

Chantel dropped her hand and stirred the grass blades beside her chair. "I'm glad you brought us here so we could see the White Horse carving," she said softly. "The horse brought me here for what he called a 'scouring.'" She looked across at Mr. Smythe.

"Yes, that's the right word," he agreed. "It means scrubbing or cleaning."

"Like scouring a frying pan after breakfast," said Owen.

"Exactly," Mr. Smythe agreed. "The carving is scrubbed clean of weeds. Do you know how often it happened?" he asked Chantel.

"Every seven years," she answered.

Mr. Smythe looked impressed.

Chantel described the Pastime Festival and how it was brought to a halt with the announcement from the Eye Maker. "After we'd learned that the red mare had been ploughed under, the White Horse said, 'You are the Magic Child. You will raise her for me. You will make Thomas's wish come true.' Then he said something I didn't understand ... " Chantel closed her eyes in an effort to remember. "'The others will help. You have all the information you need. The blacksmith will also assist.'" Chantel opened her eyes and shrugged helplessly. "Do we have to go back to Wayland?"

"He means me," said Mr. Smythe softly. "I had an early ancestor who was a blacksmith." He gave a huge grin. "Everything is linked."

Owen punched the air with delight and grinned at the others. "Told you!"

"That's not all," continued Mr. Smythe. "Lord Craven-Smythe was my relative, like Thomas is yours. My family stopped using the title and the Craven name when I was a youngster and the money ran out. Not much point being known as a lord when you can't live like one."

"You're a lord ... Wow! Do you know the queen?" said Adam, his voice full of awe.

Mr. Smythe laughed. "I've met her, but what about your links to royalty?"

Adam's eyes bulged. "Ours?"

Mr. Smythe sat up and waved his hand at the valley spread below. "You children are a part of this area. Generations of your families have lived here. King Alfred was born here. So were Alin and Thomas. I suspect that, like many people in White Horse Vale, your family tree would show links to all three of them. That might be why the White Horse could show Chantel those episodes of the past."

"So even though we were born in Canada, we might be related to King Alfred. That's wild," said Adam. He looked sideways at Owen and smirked.

Owen tossed a handful of grass at him. "If you're related, so are we."

Holly and Chantel laughed at each other, eyes shining.

Mr. Smythe rose creakily to his feet and brushed the grass from his pants. "Come on. Chop, chop! What are we waiting for?"

"Where are we going?" asked Adam.

"To Tysoe, to find the red horse. Where else?" said Mr. Smythe as he flung open the doors of the Land Rover. "We'll eat our sandwiches in the car to save time on the way."

"Just a minute. I've something to show you," said Chantel. She reached in her pocket and held out her hand. The piece of talisman glinted in the sunshine. "It was on my pillow when I woke this morning. We still need it for when we find the other half."

CHAPTER TWELVE

SIX FOR GOLD

The grassy downs flashed past and gave way to wooded hillsides. The Land Rover bucketed up and down the country lanes, slowing to pass through small villages. Several times it darted through leafy green tunnels and burst out into glorious sunshine on the crest of a hill, another valley opening out before them.

"Nearly there," Mr. Smythe called as they entered a series of steep zigzag turns that dropped them towards a small hamlet.

Owen clutched the back of the seat and yelled, "Stop!"

With a shriek of brakes the Land Rover skidded to a halt.

"What in heaven's name ...?" Mr. Smythe's voice trailed off as Owen pointed to an overgrown sign at the side of the lane.

"YOU ARE NOW ENT   THE VA   OF RE HORSE," the sign read.

Owen leapt out of the car and pulled away tendrils of ivy. The sign was cracked and peeling but the message clear: "YOU ARE NOW ENTERING THE VALE OF THE RED HORSE."

"There really is such a place," Holly said.

"Well spotted, Owen." Mr. Smythe gave a thumbs up. "That was almost worth giving me a heart attack."

Owen climbed back in and snapped on his seat belt. "Sorry, sir. I didn't mean to startle you. But it is a good find, isn't it?"

"That must be Tysoe." Chantel pointed to the cluster of roofs and a church steeple huddled in the valley below. "The red mare's on one of these hills." She gazed around.

Mr. Smythe let out the clutch and they soared downhill to stop in the parking area between the Tysoe churchyard and the Red Nag Pub.

The older cousins jumped out of the Land Rover and helped Chantel with her crutches. They gazed at the hills around the village with dismay.

"This can't be right," Chantel protested. "There are too many trees and bushes. The red mare was in a big cleared meadow. I saw her!"

"Clearings grow over," sighed Mr. Smythe. He pulled the silver box out of his bag and placed it on the hood of the Land Rover. With great care he lifted the lid, opened the old book and offered it to Chantel.

She leaned against the Land Rover and tried to read the description of the site of the horses. The words were difficult, so Holly leaned over and helped her.

"Red Horse Hill is east of Tysoe church ... with the east axis of the church pointing directly to the figure," they chanted together.

Chantel looked up. "We need a compass."

Owen flashed his explorer watch and pressed a couple of buttons. "Okay ... north's thataway."

"Then this is east." Chantel pointed to the hillside rising directly above one side of the church.

They stared at the slope.

Mr. Smythe grunted. "At least it has fewer trees than some of the other slopes." His eyes passed over the sparse woodland and glared at the small bushes and patches of open ground, as if willing the red mare to materialize.

Tears filled Chantel's eyes. "We'll never be able to find her."

Adam gave her hand a squeeze. "What if we say Wayland's rhyme? It might help, like a spell."

The cousins looked sideways at Mr. Smythe.

To their surprise he nodded briskly. "Wouldn't hurt."

"Hold hands to make a circle," suggested Chantel.

Mr. Smythe grinned. "There's five of us. That's a lucky number, like the number seven."

They linked hands and chanted quietly:

"Those you seek are running still,
Though hidden now, beneath the hill.
What lies below is seen on high.
Seek them where the magpies fly.

Seek them as small shadows, cast
By the sun when noon hath passed.
Red like white in slumber lie,
The talisman within the eye."

A breeze rippled around them, and the sun suddenly seemed to shine brighter.

Hello, child.

The familiar feeling of friendship washed over Chantel. She glanced around, but obviously no one else could hear. She thought her reply. *Horse! You're here!*

I'm always here.

Chantel gave a silent giggle. *No, I mean here at Tysoe. Can you see the red mare?*

No, there is only emptiness.

Feeling confident, Chantel smiled. *She'll come.*

At the same moment, Adam heard a whisper in his head. It seemed far away but was dark and compelling.

Adam, listen to me.

Adam looked around the circle. No one else showed signs of hearing anything, though Chantel looked happier.

Go away, Worm, thought Adam. He tried to block out the voice.

Adam, I'm strong. Come. Share my power.

You're a liar. You wanted to share power with Holly.

Of course, whispered the dragon. *She was holding the talisman. But it was you I wanted. We could be such friends, you and I. Find the missing half of the talisman and call for me. Then you and your sister will be equal. Imagine ... the girl and the horse and you and the dragon. The magic would be balanced.*

The voice faded, leaving Adam disturbed and uneasy. He glanced around the circle. No one had noticed anything. He looked down again at Chantel's rapt face. Suddenly he understood — she and the horse were talking! A flash of anger swept over him. She was going to do it again, tell everyone what to do and they'd all dance to her whims.

He dropped her hand as though it burned him.

Everyone abandoned the circle and stared back up at the hillside.

"Now what?" asked Holly.

A woman appeared in the doorway of the Red Nag. "Hello, my dears. Can I help you?" she called.

Chantel turned. "We've heard about the red horse. We were wondering where it used to be."

The woman leaned back into the pub. "George," she called. "There be people asking about yon red mare. Bring out the picture, dearie."

A sturdy farmer appeared, carrying a framed photo. "I'm George Whitfield. This be an aerial photo of my farm. It were taken some years ago by one of them archeologists, but not much has changed." He placed the photo on the hood of the Land Rover and jabbed his finger on the glass. "Here be the church, and here be yon hillside. See anything?"

Five heads pored over the photo. It took them a while to decode the unusual view of the landscape. Suddenly Chantel gave a yelp.

"The shadows. Look at the shadows! They make lines. There's a horse's head ... and ears ..." Her fingers traced a line on the surface of the glass. She turned and gazed intently at the hillside before her. "Am I dreaming? The lines are still there."

Several customers, glasses in hand, had followed George out of the pub and into the sunshine. They joined the group staring up at the hillside.

Owen danced from one foot to the other. He quoted softly, "What lies below is seen on high. Seek them where the magpies fly."

He grinned. "This is an aerial photo, a bird's-eye view, and there are the magpies."

The children looked up.

"I see one, two ... six black birds flying around up there. I can't tell if they're magpies, though ... and I can't see anything else," admitted Adam.

"Me neither," sighed Holly.

"Bet you they are." Owen squinted at the hill, his head on one side. "It's big," he said suddenly. "Really big. Chantel's right, there is something there."

"You see it too? Great." Chantel pointed, her hand trembling with excitement. "The ears start near the bushes on the top. Then the nose runs way, way down, almost to the stone wall on the left." She beamed.

Owen grinned at her and nodded.

"What are you looking at?" cried Holly.

"Magnificent. You're seeing what archeologists call crop marks." Mr. Smythe rubbed his hands together. "In a dry summer under hot sun, grass gradually bleaches paler and paler until it goes brown. Where grass grows over an area that has something underneath, like a building foundation, or the densely packed lines of a hill carving like the red mare, the roots don't get much nourishment. Those blades bleach faster than the surrounding grass.

"Look at the slope again and watch for subtle changes in color in a faint line. I'll guide you. Fix your eyes first on the little white cloud in the sky."

Adam and Holly looked up. So did the customers.

"Immediately below is a clump of bushes."

"Found them," chorused Holly and Adam.

Several customers grunted their agreement.

"Now run your eyes across the grass of the clearing below," instructed Mr. Smythe. "Watch for a pale yellow-green line running diagonally towards the left ... way down to the large tree by the wall ... then curving back ..."

"Got it," said Adam with satisfaction.

"It's a ghostly horse's head," said Holly in amazement. "It's there but it's not there."

"I'll be danged," commented a customer.

"Could we make the head show up clearer?" Owen asked.

"How?" said Holly.

"Paint the lines?" suggested Chantel.

Adam and Owen burst out laughing, but Mr. Smythe looked thoughtful. He glanced across at George Whitfield and raised his eyebrows.

George Whitfield chuckled. "You be serious? You really want to paint the old horse's head?"

"Please," said Chantel. "Then we could take a proper photo of her."

"Yes, please let us!" added the other children.

"I been asked some funny things in my time," said George, shaking his head, "but this be the strangest." He looked up at the hillside, scratching his head. "I don't reckon you should use paint. Not good for the land, see. But I have some bags of lime. You could sprinkle that along the lines, if you think it would show. I were goin' to lime yon fields anyway."

Mr. Smythe clapped George on the back as Holly and

Owen thanked him.

A fluttering movement caught Chantel's eye. Six magpies had settled on the roof of the pub. She nudged Holly and pointed. Holly squeezed her arm.

Chantel leaned against the Land Rover to rest her leg again. She closed her eyes. *Horse, you'll see her soon. I promise.*

Equus blew gently. Chantel's hair lifted.

Only Adam seemed detached from the excitement. He stood in the middle of the parking lot, caught in a whirl of emotions.

***

"Something's happening. The dragon is stirring." Ava circled around Myrddin. *"He is growing in power. The rising magic feeds him."*

Myrddin shrugged helplessly. *"We have no tools. Our power is limited. Only Equus or the boy child can stop him."*

Ava flew away to observe the dragon again.

The dragon ignored her. Once more he focused his strengthening power against the bonds of starlight surrounding him.

They held firm.

He retrieved his power and refocused. With a toothy grin, he bombarded the human boy child with anger and resentment.

Adam watched as George Whitfield backed out his farm truck and leaned out of the window to confer with Mr. Smythe. He felt strange, suddenly angry, resentful, and irritated by the excitement and activity around him.

He watched as Mr. Smythe fetched the folding chair from the back of the Land Rover and helped Chantel to sit facing the hillside. She clutched binoculars and held a cell phone in her lap.

Holly and Owen climbed into the back of George Whitfield's truck, their faces alight.

"Come on, Adam, we're picking up bags of lime. Then Mr. Whitfield will drop us off at the top of the hill," shouted Owen.

"Are you staying here or what?" called Holly.

Chantel grinned at him. She waved her phone. "Go on, Adam. I'll be fine. Mr. Smythe's got a cell phone and so have I. I'll tell you all what to do from down here."

Adam's frustration grew. There she was again! His little sister ordering everyone around. *The talisman is the key to power.* The thought appeared unbidden in his head.

Adam straightened his shoulders. That's right. If he found the other half of the talisman, then things would change. He could bargain with everyone — his parents, Chantel, the White Horse. He wouldn't need the pesky dragon! For once he would be in charge.

"Hold on. I'm coming." Adam ran and leapt up over the back of the truck. He hung over the side and called urgently to Mr. Smythe. "Please ... Can I have the other phone to coordinate with Chantel?"

"I don't see why not." Mr. Smythe handed over his cell phone and climbed into the cab.

With a scrape of gears they were off. Chantel and the customers waved and shouted encouragement.

⊠ ⊠ ⊠

Chantel watched the hill through her binoculars. The phone rang. She tucked it against her ear.

"Can you see us?" Adam's voice was clear.

The pub customers and some passersby hung around and listened. They watched the small figures silhouetted on the skyline.

"I see you," Chantel said. She waved and giggled. She couldn't help it. Several patrons were dragging chairs out of the bar. They sat down and stared at the hill.

"What's with all the people?" asked Adam.

"They're from the village." Chantel tried not to laugh. "They've come to watch."

"You bet," someone called out, and waved a glass of beer. "It's the first entertainment round these parts for weeks."

Laughter ran through the crowd.

"Oh." Adam sounded as though he didn't understand at all. "Chantel, guide me to the start of the crop mark. They're hard to spot up here. Once I'm in place I'll hand the phone to Holly. Guide her along the line to halfway; then Owen will go to the bottom. Mr. Smythe will mark our spots with scoops of lime. Then we'll connect them up."

"Cool," replied Chantel. "Like a giant dot-to-dot puzzle."

The eavesdroppers laughed again.

Chantel peered through the binoculars. "I'm watching."

"Right," said Adam. His distant figure waved. "I'll walk to

where we think the line starts. Direct me if it's not correct."

Everyone watched the small figure make his way below the clump of bushes.

"Wait ... you've gone too far," Chantel called. "Step left ... I mean right ... walk up a bit ... stop!"

Slowly she positioned the three figures along the barely visible crop mark.

"Be danged if I can see any lines. I'm going for another beer." One man lumbered to his feet and left.

Oh dear. What if my eyes are playing tricks? Chantel thought. There really is nothing much to see.

See with your inner eyes, the White Horse said. *See what Alfred saw.*

I'll try, Chantel thought.

Suddenly Mr. Smythe's voice came over the phone. "Chantel, we're going to join the line. It'll take a while, so you can switch off."

"Good luck," Chantel called back. She pressed the switch and watched through the binoculars.

Bit by bit a white line grew across the hillside.

"Here, dearie." The woman from the pub appeared with a glass of cold lemonade. "It's hot work sitting in the sun. Drink up and don't look so worried. Everyone's having the time of their life. You lot should come every week. It's right good for business."

Chantel looked around. The car park was full. Children were swinging on the church gate and sitting on the wall. A couple of women jiggled strollers containing sleeping babies, and several people had brought their own folding chairs. The entire village had turned out to watch.

Step by careful step, the lines made sense. Long thin lines with gentle curves suggested a nose and the neck. Four short lines made pointed ears.

"Well, I'll be blowed," said a customer. "The old mare's still watching over us. Who'd have believed it."

The audience began to clap.

The six magpies called, spread their wings and flapped slowly towards the hill.

<hr/>

Mr. Smythe, Holly, Owen, and Adam heard the clapping and looked proudly over their handiwork.

"It doesn't look like a horse from up here," said Holly, "but it must from down there." She gave a wave.

"It doesn't feel right," said Owen. He stood between the lines, frowning. "Something's missing."

"Most of the horse," Holly pointed out. "We've only found the head. The rest is too overgrown."

"Gotta find the eye," Adam muttered. He walked around the sloping ground searching for clues. "The Eye Maker put white chalk in the eye."

Mr. Smythe looked doubtful. "I know Chantel told us about a white eye, but I never found any reference to it in my research. This is a big figure. We'd have to dig up half the area to locate the eye."

Owen shook his head. "Not if she's mate to the White Horse." He gestured towards the lines on the ground. "She's the same design, isn't she?"

"There are similarities," Mr. Smythe agreed.

"Then I think I know how to find the eye," Owen said.

"Go on," encouraged Mr. Smythe.

Owen's eyes danced. "It's that magic number thing again. Seven steps from the ear of the White Horse to the top of its eye. I bet it's the same for the red mare."

"Great!" Adam grabbed the trowel they used for scooping lime. He ran to the center of the head. "You pace. I'll dig."

"More magic. Why not?" shrugged Mr. Smythe. A shadow flitted over his face. He looked up. The magpies were circling overhead. "Six for gold," he muttered. "I wonder ..."

Owen paced. Holly counted.

Adam crouched down and rammed the trowel through the tangled grass. He dug feverishly in the reddish brown dirt. It was hard work and he had to dig deep.

"I see some white flecks," he said finally.

"Oh ye of little faith," Mr. Smythe said to himself, shaking his head.

He, Holly and Owen dashed over to watch.

Adam scrabbled and scraped. The trowel jarred in his hand. Anxiously he pushed the others out of the way.

"Watch out," he grunted as he forced the trowel down into the hard-packed chalk and leaned on it with all his might.

⧆ ⧆ ⧆

Puzzled questions floated among the watchers in the car park.

"What are they doing?"

"They're in a huddle. Is someone hurt?"

"Do you know what's going on, lassie?"

Chantel glued her eyes to the binoculars. Excitement

tingled from her toes, up her spine, and electrified the hairs on her head. She watched the magpies fly in closer and closer circles until they were directly over Adam.

Six for gold, Horse, she thought. *Watch carefully.*

I'm watching, replied the White Horse.

With a scatter of debris, the packed chalk suddenly gave way and something shiny flew through the air.

Hands shot out.

Adam dropped the trowel and lunged forward. He grabbed the gold fragment and clutched it to his chest with a shout of triumph.

The magpies gave several piercing cries and disappeared over the hilltop.

The huddle on the hillside broke apart as the children and Mr. Smythe ran beyond the lines so the people below could see.

"The eye! They found the eye," Chantel shouted. Adam was dancing up and down, waving his hand in the air. There was a flash as the sun caught the other piece of talisman.

The crowd hooted and hollered.

Horse, Chantel called inside her head. *Adam's found the rest of the talisman!*

The cell phone rang, interrupting her. "Don't tell anyone down there what I found," Adam whispered.

"'Course not," Chantel replied.

Adam's voice became triumphant. "What a day! We're coming down!"

"Well, I be danged. There be the red mare's head, as clear as day." George Whitfield gazed in amazement. "'Tis many a year since she watched over us! This calls for a celebration. Betsy, bring out food and drinks."

The car park became the site of an instant party. Food appeared as if by magic, and everyone toasted the reappearance of the red mare with pints of beer or bottles of lemonade.

A great cheer went up as Adam, Holly, Owen, and Mr. Smythe appeared through the trees.

At the height of the celebration, Chantel tried to reach the White Horse. *Did we find enough of your beautiful red mare?* she asked.

You did. The people believe in her again, now she looks over the vale. Soon she will join me and we will once more ride the wind together, replied the White Horse.

We couldn't find the foal, Chantel added sadly.

It matters not. When the red mare runs, the foal will follow. Thank you, Magic Child. Your task is almost complete. All that is left is for you and Adam to make the talisman whole.

Chantel sensed another presence approaching.

She comes. Now we can ride the wind together!

The excited whicker of two horses greeting sounded in Chantel's head. She felt the red mare's friendly curiosity and gratitude mingle with the familiar feelings from the White Horse. Tears of joy pricked behind her eyes as she listened to the fading echo of a double set of hoof beats.

CHAPTER THIRTEEN

POWER STRUGGLES

The village party continued into the evening, but a pall had fallen over the children.

Adam would not let the piece of talisman out of his sight.

"Can I see it?" Chantel whispered.

He flashed a tantalizing glimpse.

Chantel held out her hand, but he shook his head and replaced the gold in his pocket. Adam could feel the power of the talisman. It throbbed, warming him and strengthening his resolve. For once he felt in total control. He owned a piece of magic and he was going to use it.

He refused to let anyone else handle it.

"Got to keep it safe," Adam said firmly. He wouldn't even show it to Mr. Smythe.

The drive back to White Horse Farm was tense.

The fight erupted at bedtime. The three cousins confronted Adam in his bedroom.

"Adam Maxwell, stop being a pain," said Holly. "So you found the other half of the talisman. That doesn't make you the big cheese."

"Yeah! It doesn't even belong to you," added Owen. "It belongs to the White Horse."

Chantel looked worried. "Why won't you let us look at it? You can't keep it forever. We've promised to fix it."

"Who says?" retorted Adam. "Finders keepers."

Chantel's, Holly's, and Owen's jaws dropped.

"You wouldn't dare ... We have to make the talisman whole," Chantel stammered.

"Why? So the horse can gallop off with it?" Adam answered. "Well, maybe I want to use it first."

"You've been talking to that dragon again," Owen accused.

"I'm not talking to any stupid dragon, pathetic horse, know-it-all cousins, or crazy sister. You're just jealous," Adam flung back. He grabbed his PJs and turned to leave.

Goaded beyond endurance, Owen tackled Adam's knees and brought him to the floor. The boys hammered at each other. Holly scrambled up onto the top bunk; Chantel cowered in the corner, trying to protect her leg with the crutches.

"I hate you, Adam," she yelled. "You're spoiling everything!"

The door opened. "Owen ... Adam ... Behave!" roared Uncle Ron. He pointed to the girls. "You two, into your own room and get ready for bed."

Silently, Holly climbed down and Chantel hobbled past

her uncle as the boys scrambled to their feet.

Uncle Ron glared at the boys. "You know the rule ... no fighting no matter what. Owen, get your duvet and pillow. You can sleep in the study tonight."

"But, Dad ... I ... That's not fair."

His father pointed to the door.

Owen did as he was told, gathering his night things together in silence. He stomped out.

Uncle Ron looked at Adam. "Get into bed and never let me see you fighting again."

❈ ❈ ❈

The dragon chortled as Adam's anger coursed once more through his veins.

Ava shuddered and left her post to report to Myrddin. "The dragon is manipulating the boy's thoughts again."

Myrddin spread his hands in despair. "We cannot interfere. The boy must choose freely. His heart is his own."

"Join with me, Myrddin. Keep hope alive while Equus rides the wind. Send peaceful thoughts to Gaia." Ava spread her wings in blessing.

Myrddin shook out his cloak and flung stardust towards the misty blue planet.

❈ ❈ ❈

Adam seethed in his bunk, wondering how to get both halves of the talisman.

He turned over in bed, replaying in his head the magical

"clang" of Wayland's anvil and the image of the two halves coming together. He banged his head several times on the pillow. "Think, brain, think! How can I get the other half from Chantel, then get to Wayland's Smithy on my own?" he said to himself.

Slipping his hand under his pillow, Adam touched his piece of the talisman to reassure himself that it was still safe. He let go quickly, not wanting to fall asleep holding it. He did not want to talk to the dragon until the talisman was whole and he had something to bargain with. A thought occurred to him. What if he held it just long enough to make a tiny wish?

Adam clasped the gold piece and closed his eyes. "I wish there was a way to get the other half of the talisman from Chantel," he whispered, and let go, removing his hand from under the pillow.

No bright ideas occurred to him.

The bedroom seemed empty and unfriendly. Adam's thoughts drifted towards Owen sleeping on the study couch. Served Owen right for fighting!

It was a long time before he slept.

❈ ❈ ❈

Holly and Chantel lay talking quietly.

"We've got to take both halves of the talisman to Wayland's Smithy," said Chantel. "We promised the White Horse we'd make it whole."

"We will," soothed Holly.

"Adam won't let us." Chantel's voice broke in a little

sob. "He hates me again, like he did in Canada."

Holly stuck her hand between the beds and held Chantel's hand. "He doesn't really hate you. He's just messed up with the divorce stuff. But know what?"

"What?" sniffed Chantel.

"Adam will come through when he has to. He did when I was captured by the dragon."

"You're not his sister," muttered Chantel. "He likes you."

"You'll see," said Holly sleepily.

⊠ ⊠ ⊠

Owen lay stiffly on his back. Adam Maxwell's the know-it-all, not me, he thought. Well, game over. I'm not helping him anymore. I'm going to help Mr. Smythe instead. He said I could work with him excavating what's left of the red mare so she will be there forever.

Thinking about the reappearance of the red mare brought a smile to Owen's lips. He burrowed into the soft couch cushions and went to sleep.

⊠ ⊠ ⊠

At dawn, a blackbird perched on the thatch and burst into song. Adam awoke and pulled the pillow over his ears. The song penetrated through the stuffing. He sat up, cussed and headed for the bathroom.

As he turned on the tap to wash his hands, Adam stared in disbelief. There beside the soap was Chantel's half of the talisman.

"Chantel must have dropped it by mistake." Adam grinned. "Tough luck, Tootsie." He palmed the talisman and raced back to his bedroom.

Retrieving his piece from under the pillow, Adam butted the two halves together. He could feel a current running between them. He threw on his clothes, tucked the pieces in the pocket of his jean jacket and zipped it shut. Shoes in hand, he tiptoed downstairs and let himself out of the back door.

He slipped into his shoes, ran to the barn and saddled up Mischief. "Come on, girl," he whispered. "Time for a morning ride." He led Mischief out of the far door of the barn into the paddock so no one in the house would hear hooves on the cobbles. She let Adam mount without trouble. They trotted over the grass towards the gate in the far corner. Adam dismounted, opened it and led Mischief through. The gate squeaked.

❋ ❋ ❋

Holly awoke with a start, unsure why. Then she heard the noise again. A distant squeal of metal against metal. It sounded like the paddock gate. She slipped from her bed and looked out of the window.

Adam was on the far side of the paddock gate, trying to mount Mischief.

Holly dodged behind the curtain and watched through a gap. He was too busy coping with Mischief to worry about the noise from the gate. Once again his pony was living up to her name. She danced around in circles. Stuck with one foot in a stirrup, Adam hopped around after her, unable to spring up.

Serves him right, thought Holly gleefully. She tiptoed out of her bedroom and crept into the study.

"Owen, wake up." Holly gently shook his shoulder. "Adam's up to something. He and Mischief are sneaking out of the paddock."

Owen sat up. He rubbed his eyes, scratched his scalp and tried to concentrate. "Where's he going?"

Holly shrugged. "Dunno, but I could make a guess."

"Wayland's Smithy," they chorused softly.

"Let's follow him." Owen slid from under the duvet and grabbed his clothes.

"What about Chantel? She can't ride with her leg in a cast."

"Okay. I'll take Batman. You and Chantel come with Harlequin and the pony trap. Dad asked Mr. O'Reilly to clean it up for us yesterday. It's all ready to go."

Holly gave a thumbs up and left to wake Chantel.

Owen dressed swiftly and headed downstairs. He paused to scribble a note: "Gone for an early ride along the Ridgeway. We'll get our own breakfast when we come back." Leaving the note on the table, he slipped outside.

⬧ ⬧ ⬧

Adam rode the lanes, watching for the road to Wayland's Smithy. He was nervous about Mischief's hoofs waking people, but he didn't dare go by the fields as he didn't know the way.

He relaxed as he passed several racehorses being exercised.

The neighbors were used to hoof beats in the early morning. He wiped the beads of perspiration from his brow. No one had tried to stop him from leaving the farm, and now he was on the correct track. Things were looking good.

⊠ ⊠ ⊠

Owen and Batman worked in rhythm. They galloped across a field. Then Batman stood while Owen slid off to unlatch the gate. Batman stepped through and stood again while Owen shut the gate and remounted. Then they were off, racing across the next field.

By the fifth gate their movements had become a fluid dance. Finally they were clear of the fields and on the long woodland gallop that paralleled part of the Ridgeway.

Owen reined in behind a thicket. He and Batman were breathing heavily.

"We must be ahead of Adam," Owen whispered as he stroked Batman's neck. "He doesn't know the shortcuts." He dismounted, tethered Batman loosely to a tree and gave him a pat. "Be good. I'll be back soon."

He picked his way through the wood until he was within sight of the Ridgeway. Dropping to the ground, he wriggled under a concealing bush and waited.

Five minutes later, Adam and Mischief trotted past.

⊠ ⊠ ⊠

"Go fast, Holly," pleaded Chantel. She was in a blind panic after discovering the loss of her piece of talisman. She clutched the side of the pony trap, willing it to fly.

Holly shook her head. She held Harlequin at a steady trot. "We can't gallop. It's dangerous. The trap could hit a bump and overturn. We're going as fast as we can."

Chantel subsided unhappily.

⊠ ⊠ ⊠

Adam dismounted, rubbed his sweaty palms on his jeans and led Mischief into the enclosure of Wayland's Smithy. He took his time closing the gate and knotting the reins safely up around the horse's neck. Finally he gathered enough courage to stand between the magical beech trees and survey the barrow. It looked peaceful and unthreatening in the early morning sunlight. Adam stepped forward into the circle.

Stillness fell, no leaves rustled, no bird sang. Only his heart thumped as he tiptoed across the grass.

The great gray stones loomed before him.

Adam stooped beneath the lintel and peered inside. Tendrils of magic wafted out to greet him.

"Er ... Wayland," he called, his voice thin and uneasy. "It's me, Adam. I've brought the talisman for you to fix."

A flame flickered deep in the darkness.

"ENTER."

Bile rose in Adam's throat. He couldn't do it. He could not enter that black passage on his own. No matter what the stakes or how hard the magic pulled, his fear of dark enclosed spaces overcame it. He sank to his knees.

A horse whickered and Mischief answered. Adam glanced back.

Owen appeared between the beech trees.

Adam gasped and flung himself into the entrance of the barrow.

⊠ ⊠ ⊠

Darkness pressed down, a smothering blackness that made Adam gasp and pant with fear. He fought through it, hand by hand, knee by knee, driven by his need for the talisman. Finally the passage widened and a pulsing crimson glow gave enough light to see.

Adam rose to his feet and stumbled into a great cavern lit by a glowing forge. A gigantic man appeared and disappeared in clouds of smoke and steam as he worked at the anvil. Behind him, half hidden in the shadows, was a red mare.

Adam stopped in shock. He looked around guiltily, but there was no sign of the White Horse.

The blacksmith lifted his face and Adam got his second shock. The face was familiar.

"Mr. S ... S ... Smythe!" Adam gasped, then clapped his hands over his ears as Wayland's hammer arm rose and fell, pounding a glowing horseshoe. Steam hissed as he dunked it into a pail of water.

Clasping the horseshoe in long black pincers, Wayland turned to the shadows and the red mare lifted her hoof. Thick yellow smoke obscured them as Wayland straddled her leg and clapped the horseshoe in place.

The acrid smell of singeing assailed Adam's nose and throat as he watched the magic of fire, water, and iron at work on the hoof.

Wayland slapped the red mare's rear and she dropped her foot. He peered at Adam through the smoke and gestured towards his anvil.

"LAY THE PIECES DOWN."

Adam unzipped his pocket and dropped the two gold pieces on the anvil.

"LOOK DEEP IN THY HEART AS I JOIN THE PARTS."

Wayland scooped the halves onto a shovel and thrust it into the heart of the furnace. After a few seconds he pulled it out, tipped the glowing fragments onto the anvil and lifted his hammer.

CLANG! A sound as if a thousand hammers struck at the same time. A million sparks swirled around the cavern and Adam swirled with them.

He whirled through space and time, seeing snatches of everything happening around him.

Owen was at the entry of the barrow, kicking the stones. Adam laughed.

Holly was driving the pony trap up the Ridgeway. Chantel sat in the back, clutching the sides and peering ahead. Adam smirked, ignoring a twinge of guilt. He'd outwitted Chantel!

CLANG! The hammer fell again. The sparks whirled Adam higher.

Uncle Ron and Auntie Lynne were sharing a pot of tea and reading a note. Fleetingly, Adam hoped they weren't worried.

He swirled above Mr. Smythe crouched over the kitchen table, painstakingly charting the red mare's crop lines. Guilt tweaked Adam again. He'd found the missing piece of the talisman through Mr. Smythe's help, and then been rude to him.

The golden sparks danced him away. Halfway around the world he saw his parents sleeping — in separate rooms. His father slept in Adam's bed.

Adam roared with anger, "Get out! That's my room!"

CLANG! The sparks circled upward towards an answering roar from the stars.

A silvery net floated in darkness. In it was the dragon.

The dragon was swollen with power. He thrust again and again against the shimmering netting and roared with triumph as one claw finally sliced through and ripped the net apart.

Speechless with horror, Adam looked on as the dragon flew through the sky and plucked Chantel from the pony trap.

"NOOOooo," yelled Adam. His voice came from the bottom of his heart and echoed through the universe. "Leave her alone. Stop making things bad things happen."

He was back in the cavern.

Wayland stood beside the anvil holding up the talisman, made whole.

The dragon symbol faced Adam.

Wayland pointed to the furnace.

Adam stared at a vision within the flames.

The dragon leered at them from the top of Dragon Hill, a terrified Chantel in his clutches.

Wayland turned the talisman. The horse symbol appeared.

Wind rushed through the cavern as the White Horse galloped in and stopped beside Wayland. The Red Mare stepped forward to join him.

They too stared at the dragon vision in the flames.

Adam sprinted across the cavern floor and leapt up to pull on Wayland's arm.

"Stop it. Say it's only pictures, that you're making everything happen! Give the talisman to me. I'll make it stop."

Wayland brushed Adam off as though he were a fly. "ENTER," he boomed.

Adam turned.

Holly and Owen scrambled out of the passage and into the cavern.

Wayland dropped his arm and handed the talisman to Adam.

Immediately the cavern filled with whispers. Adam could hear thoughts.

Good. The boy holds the talisman. He feels its power. He will never be able to refuse it now. And I have a hostage. The dragon cackled in triumph. *Soon the horse will be banished.*

Adam will never save me. What shall I do? despaired Chantel. Her mind cast around desperately for ways to extract herself from the dragon.

This is all Adam's fault, thought Holly. *Thank goodness the horse is here.*

Adam staggered as a wave of disgust from Holly hit him. His anger flared.

He staggered again as the sheer wordless force of Owen's anger was directed towards him. He returned it.

In the flames the dragon laughed and flexed his muscles.

Poor humans. They do not understand how it all works, murmured an unfamiliar voice in Adam's mind. Adam swung around and looked uncomprehendingly into the sad eyes of the Red Mare.

Only the thoughts of Wayland and the White Horse were veiled.

Adam held the talisman up and called aloud, "Stop! Stop everything."

The whispers stilled.

"The talisman is mine," shouted Adam. "I brought the halves to Wayland and asked him to join them."

"THE TALISMAN IS THINE," Wayland agreed.

"But I don't want bad things to happen." Adam's voice trembled.

"YOUR HEART SWAYS THE TALISMAN'S WAYS," said Wayland.

Owen opened his mouth to say something cutting, but Holly stood on his foot. She gestured towards Adam.

Once more Adam was riveted by the vision in the flames.

Adam had read the hate in Owen's mind, and returned it. Immediately the dragon had grown. The same thing had happened when he'd reacted angrily to Holly's disgust. The dragon had grown.

"It really is the hate, isn't it?" Adam frantically tried to make sense of it all. "Hate and anger make the dragon grow! The dragon said it, but I didn't understand. He feeds on anger and hate ... and the talisman ..." Adam struggled to understand the connection. "It sort of strengthened the link between us, so he could feed better?"

The White Horse nodded. *The talisman works in many ways. It will magnify emotions.*

Adam looked anxiously into the flames again.

Clutching Chantel in one claw, the dragon was digging viciously into the scar on Dragon Hill with the other. A small dark hole appeared. He roared with triumph and began to widen it.

"All emotions?" Adam's voice grew shrill. "I'd have to stop thinking! But brains think. That's what they do!" He swung around to the horse, his eyes wide. "But you don't get angry, do you? You're the only one who can use the talisman properly!"

Adam turned back to the vision in the flames as the dragon finished widening the hole and dangled Chantel over it.

"Stop hating," he yelled at Holly and Owen. "It feeds the dragon. Try doing the opposite."

Adam scrunched up his eyes, shut out the dragon's mind and concentrated on his little sister. He remembered the day she was brought home from the hospital and how her tiny hand had grasped his little finger. He remembered trying to teach her to throw a ball. She had chuckled and staggered towards him with the ball clasped to her chest. He remembered how she'd watched at the window for him to come home from school. He realized how scared she was, and sent her a stream of love and affection. He felt Owen and Holly do the same. He opened his eyes and stared anxiously into the flames.

The dragon had deflated. He was shaking his head as though to clear it and his movements seemed weaker.

"Chantel!" screamed Adam. "The horse will save you." He pressed the talisman to the forehead of the White Horse. The talisman glowed. Equus leapt from the cavern and disappeared.

Everyone watched the vision in the flames.

With a roar, the dragon dropped Chantel into the pit.

As she fell, the White Horse appeared in the vision. He leapt into the opening and sprang from it with Chantel clinging to his back. He landed on the edge of the plateau and turned to face the dragon.

The dragon reared back on his haunches with a great cry.

Horse and dragon locked eyes. The talisman gleamed on the horse's forehead. Nothing happened.

The watchers in the cavern held their breath.

Finally, the dragon cringed, belly to the earth, and began to edge backward, inch by inch. He retreated without a sound as Equus stepped delicately forward, one hoof at a time.

"Look at Chantel," whispered Holly.

The Magic Child had one arm raised and one finger pointed in the ancient sign of banishment. Silhouetted against the sun, her features were invisible. The slow-moving tableau looked like the picture of St. George and the Dragon.

The tip of the red tail reached the rim of the pit. It slipped over the edge. His eyes still locked with the horse's, the dragon's body slid slowly after his tail and silently disappeared.

Equus tapped the rim seven times with one hoof. The white scar healed over.

"What, no fight?" gasped Owen.

"It was a mind fight." Adam's voice was full of awe. "Yes!" He punched the air in triumph and grabbed the massive iron pail of water from beside Wayland's anvil. With superhuman strength he flung the contents into the furnace. "Take that, Worm."

The water hit the fire, dowsed the flames and plunged them all into darkness.

A great guffaw from Wayland filled the cavern.

The laughter boomed. The children cowered, buffeted by the sound. They clapped their hands over their ears and rocked to and fro in agony.

The laughter lessened. "Humans always surprise me," said Wayland with a chuckle.

A flint struck a spark and the great bellows blew the furnace back to life. Still chuckling, Wayland turned the bellows towards the children. A burst of air tumbled them down the passage. A third wheeze from the giant's bellows shot them out of the mouth of the barrow to sprawl on the grass in a daze.

Chantel was there to greet them. She hobbled over the grass and threw her arms around her brother.

CHAPTER FOURTEEN

SEVEN FOR A SECRET

It was seven minutes after midnight.

Chantel, Adam, Holly, and Owen were sitting on Chantel's bed, whispering. The curtains were open. They could see White Horse Hill clearly in the distance.

It was a magical night. The moon bathed the valley in brittle light.

"I'm tired, but I can't sleep. My body's all jumpy," Owen said.

"Mine too," said Chantel.

"The air's electric." Adam rubbed his hand over his hair and his red curls stood on end.

It was seven minutes after midnight, at full moon.

"The world is holding its breath," Holly murmured.

"It's waiting for the horses." Chantel tilted her head and listened. A smile lit up her face. "They're coming ... I hear them." She swung her cast off the bed, hopped to the window and leaned out over the ledge. The other children followed.

It was seven minutes after midnight, at full moon, in the seventh month.

The Great White Horse galloped along the Milky Way. The Red Mare and her foal followed. They landed on White Horse Hill and gazed at the children hanging out of the window. The Red Mare nudged her foal forward. The foal skittered and danced around her.

"Aaah," said the children.

"I'm glad you're here again!" said Chantel, aloud this time.

We're always here, replied the Great White Horse, his words unspoken, but now all four children could hear his thoughts. The talisman glinted on his forehead. *Come. It's time to ride the wind.*

Chantel and Adam found themselves on his back. Adam grasped his little sister around her waist and hung on for dear life.

Owen, with Holly behind, grinned from the back of the Red Mare.

The White Horse struck the ground seven times with his hoof. Hind muscles bunched and the two horses leapt for the stars, closely followed by the foal. They galloped among moonbeams, jumped over sunsets, hurtled through galaxies and finally cantered across the crystal sands in the Place Beyond Morning.

I must share a secret with you, said Equus as they stopped. *Can your eyes see the others?*

Hazy forms shimmered towards them across the crystal sands.

The children covered their eyes and peeped through the cracks between their fingers.

"Myrddin, Ava, you are too bright," called Equus. He spoke aloud for the first time.

The shimmering dimmed and resolved into two shapes.

A red-haired, red-bearded man strode towards them. He was wrapped in a dark cloak. As he moved, the cloak swirled with hidden colors. Beside him glided a woman with a bird headdress. Or was it a bird with a woman's body? The children couldn't tell. They gazed in awe at the silver and ebony feathers that covered her and framed her hawk-like features.

"Meet Myrddin and Ava. My true name is Equus. We are three of the Wise Ones," said Equus.

Myrddin and Ava bowed.

"Greetings," boomed Myrddin. "Ages have passed since last we met with believers. Welcome."

"Blessings for restoring the talisman to Equus." Ava raised her wings in salutation. She towered over the children.

They shrank back.

"Forgive me. I had forgotten how I seem to humans." Ava refolded her wings and smiled.

"You ... you are beautiful," stammered Owen.

Ava nodded regally. "Thank you, child." She turned. "Come, we must show you something no human has ever seen."

The horses followed, carrying the children across the sands and along a barely visible trail up the steep cliffs of glass. They stopped at the top and looked across a hidden valley.

Above them, seven magpies circled.

Holly counted. "Seven for a secret never been told," she whispered.

Below them lay the silver citadel.

Its walls still shone, but their tops were blackened by fire. The golden gates at the entrance lay shattered and twisted. Beyond the citadel the land was shrouded in mist.

A great sadness filled the children.

"What happened?" whispered Holly. "Was there a war?"

"That is the work of the Dark Being. She attempted to seize our tools of power," rumbled Myrddin.

"We evacuated the citadel, then hid our magic tools in a distant place called Gaia, that you call Earth. We thought if no one used magical powers, the Dark Being would feel less threatened and return to her own place in peace."

"And did she?" asked Adam.

The Wise Ones sadly shook their heads.

"She vowed to search to the ends of time until she found the tools," said Equus. He sighed. "She has searched without pause, for eons, and now has entered your universe."

The children's eyes widened.

Ava gently touched the tip of one wing to each fore-head. "Fear not. We will not let the Dark Being destroy your world."

"We wish to retrieve the tools from Gaia," Myrddin said. His eyes burned fiercely. "But your people have forgotten us. No one recognized our voices or understood the star messages."

"I heard Equus," said Chantel.

Myrddin's face softened. "So you did, child. Because of you, his talisman is found."

"So ... so ... you need help ... finding other tools?" asked Adam.

"Yes." Ava's reply hung in the air.

The children looked at each other and gave nods of agreement.

"We'll help," they chorused.

Ava spread her wings and gave a rapturous cry. "Yes! Yes! Yes!" Her voice echoed around the valley.

Myrddin beamed. His red hair and beard crackled with sparks and the hidden colors in his cloak danced.

Unnoticed by the children, the mist beyond the silver citadel thinned.

"Thank you, thank you," repeated Myrddin. "Help is strongest when freely offered."

Equus tossed his mane. "Chantel and Adam, Owen and Holly, you are bright and brave. You listen to your hearts. You can indeed help us. But finding our tools means waking Old Magic. As our magic stirs so does the Dark Magic."

"Like the dragon." Adam gave a shudder. "He nearly got me, and Holly and Chantel."

"Yes, like the dragon," agreed Equus. "Light and dark. There can be no light without the dark."

"Won't you help us? You saved Chantel," said Holly.

"We will help with the magic, but we cannot interfere in the ways of your people," Myrddin said.

"You mean ..." Adam struggled to understand. "You mean ... we can fly with the White Horse and fight with the dragon and stuff like that, but you can't stop Mom and Dad arguing and getting a divorce?"

Myrddin nodded. "We can only offer a feeling of warmth and peace around them."

"Or send feelings of anger and hate," said Adam ruefully. "Like the dragon sent to me."

"But you listened to your heart, Adam. In the end the dragon had no power over you." Myrddin smiled.

"There is no shame in refusing, if the task seems daunting," said Ava gently. "Do you need to reconsider?"

The children exchanged glances and shook their heads.

"Are you kidding?" Adam grinned. "Pass up a holiday full of magic? No way!"

"Magic friends," said Chantel, stroking the White Horse's neck.

"Magic adventures," added Owen.

"A summer of magic," breathed Holly.

"Will that be time enough?" Myrddin whispered to Ava.

"Traa dy liooar? We must hope it will," replied Ava.

"Your night is slipping away. I must return you," said Equus. "The journey is long so sleep and dream, sleep and dream. Ahead are your new tomorrows."

He and the Red Mare leapt for the wind.

"Watch for the star messages," called Ava.

"We will." The children waved back.

"Then farewell. We will meet again."

Auᴛʜᴏʀ's ᑎoᴛᴇ

Though *The White Horse Talisman* is a fantasy, it was inspired by a real English landscape. As a child growing up in England, I was fascinated by pictures of the three-thousand-year-old carving of the Uffington White Horse and always wondered who carved it and why. When I was ten I read *Sun Horse, Moon Horse* by Rosemary Sutcliffe and vowed that one day I would see the carved horse for myself. It never happened, and I grew up and emigrated to Canada. Five years ago, my husband decided it was time my dream was fulfilled. He organized a visit to Uffington. The horse was beautiful. We marveled at its flowing shape and massive size, and both of us circled the eye seven times. (I won't tell you what I wished for.) We were intrigued to discover that the Great White Horse wasn't the only wonder in the area. It was surrounded by other fascinating ancient sites.

My husband discovered the Blowing Stone Inn, so we stayed there, found the Blowing Stone and blew it. We walked the Ridgeway track, explored the ditches and ramparts of Uffington Castle and climbed Dragon Hill, where tradition says St. George slew the dragon. It really is bald on top! One evening we hiked to

Wayland's Smithy and entered the beech-tree circle at sunset. The magic of the place curled around me. As I stooped to crawl under the lintel stone, I saw a silver coin, an offering to Wayland, tucked in a crack. I knew then I had to write about everything I'd seen.

The story research led me on a fascinating journey through books on Celts and Saxons, paintings of saints, dragons and white horses, folksongs and folktales, children's rhymes, and other folklore. The description of the ritual scouring and the Pastime is based on the work of writer Thomas Hughes, who lived in Uffington and recorded the customs of White Horse Vale in his book *The Scouring of the White Horse*. I've stayed true to the scouring except for one detail. I needed to link the Red Mare and White Horse, so I invented the role of the eye maker and the bucket of chalk that was carried to the the Red Mare. I grieve for the lost Red Horses of Tysoe. They were ploughed over by an angry landowner in the 1800s. Their ghostly images were last seen through crop marks and aerial photos in 1968. They are now irretrievably grown over — except in stories!

As a child, I chanted the magpie rhyme many times. It's one of the oldest rhymes in the English language. The number seven is a "magic number" in many cultures, including those of the British Isles. The wealth of folkloric material and ancient sites inspired me so thoroughly that this story became not one fantasy but the first of four. You will be able to follow Chantel and Adam, Holly and Owen through the United Kingdom's mystical landscape in three more volumes of the Summer of Magic Quartet.

Andrea Spalding
August 2001

Award-winning author Andrea Spalding has written many popular books for children, including juvenile novels *Finders Keepers* and *An Island of My Own*, Young Readers *Phoebe and the Gypsy* and *The Keeper and the Crows* and picture books *Sarah May and the New Red Dress*, *Me and Mr. Mah* and *It's Raining, It's Pouring*. An accomplished storyteller, Andrea hails from England, where she was long steeped in ancient lore, lore that now finds its full expression in the first volume of the Summer of Magic Quartet. She now lives with her husband on Pender Island, BC.